Renew onli~
www.libr~
or by phoning
Bristol

D1382011

PLEASE RETURN BOOK ~~E STAMPED

GEOFFREY PHILP

UNCLE OBADIAH AND THE ALIEN

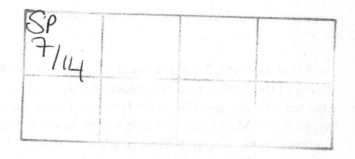

PEEPAL TREE

First published in Great Britain in 1997
Peepal Tree Press Ltd
17 King's Avenue
Leeds LS6 1QS
England
Reprinted 2007

ISBN 1 900715 01 5
ISBN 13: 9781900715010

For Judith, Bill, Alex, and Aleisha

Give thanks to Phyllis Washington who allowed me to test many of these stories on her students; Preston Allen who gave me so many good ideas for revision; Lester Goran and Evelyn Wilde Mayerson who gave me the encouragement to continue; and, of course, Erika Smilowitz-Waters and *The Caribbean Writer* for publishing several of these stories.

"Uncle Obadiah and the Alien" reprinted by permission from the *Mississippi Review*, Vol. 24, No. 3

 Peepal Tree gratefully acknowledges Arts Council support

CONTENTS

UNCLE OBADIAH AND THE ALIEN

Every summer I used to look forward to going down to me Uncle Obadiah farm in Struie. Him had me doing all kinda thing on the farm: tying out the goats, feeding the chickens, and helping with the cows. I enjoy doing the chores, for it help to get me mind off school. Uncle Obadiah make me do all these things because although him did expect me to pass the "O" levels in England, him said a man should always have something to fall back on and farming was the best work a man could do.

So one Saturday evening as I was standing on the barbecue and pulling the tarpaulin over Uncle Obadiah six foot statue of Haile Selassie, I hear ching, ching, ching, chingeleng, pang, pengeleleng, peng. I figure it was the Chinese people down the lane giving a name to they latest baby. Uncle Obadiah said Chinese people name they children by throwing a twenty-five cent piece through the window and the first sound the coin make, that's what the child name. But this was too loud for a twenty-five cent piece.

I make sure the tarpaulin was on real tight, for although a Rastaman not supposed to attach to material possessions, I know that if even a speck of dew did settle on Uncle Obadiah statue, there would be hell to pay.

I run down the gully, and see this thing that look like a black Volkswagen minibus, but it never have no window. A cloud of smoke trail from the sky down to the back. At first I think it was a army helicopter, but it didn't have no propeller. It look like a long, black metal gas tank, like something from NASA or a Russian Sputnik. But when the door open, I see something with space suit, laser gun and everything.

Well, the minute me eye clap on this thing, I take off up the hill straight to Uncle Obadiah for him was the only one who would believe me. But when me get to him house, even him didn't believe me.

"After that arse-tearing yu father give yu last week for telling lies, yu still doing it?" him said.

"I not telling lies anymore," I said. And I guess by the look on me face, him decide to believe me.

So him put on him Wellingtons and come down the gully with me. By then the alien was trying to come out of the spaceship. When Uncle Obadiah see the alien, him spliff drop right out of him mouth.

It had long, wiry brown hair, big black eyes, and horrible crooked teeth. I was going throw some rockstones at it when Uncle Obadiah discern why the thing looking so ugly. It was the dead stamp of Margaret Thatcher. No wonder it looked so evil, and if we did know better, we would have sent it packing right there. Uncle Obadiah stand up on the side of the gully and look down at the alien.

"Wha de raas yu doing in me herb field? Yu killing off all me herb plant," said Uncle Obadiah.

The alien said, "Terribly sorry, my dear fellow, but I appear to be stuck. But don't worry, I'll have it fixed in a minute."

The alien was trying to get it foot out of the door, and when Uncle Obadiah see that, him do what any Rastaman would do, him go down the gully to help out a fellow being.

The two of them rocked the spaceship, but still the alien couldn't come out, so Uncle Obadiah call me down. At first, I never want to go, but Uncle Obadiah tell me that everything was all right.

Night was coming fast, and we could barely see each other, which was good, because who would want to look at a thing as ugly as that in the dark? We rocked the spaceship again, and the alien pull him foot out the door.

Then the alien turn to Uncle Obadiah to thank him, see him

face, and said, "Menelik?" and that's when the friendship start. For Uncle Obadiah realize that this was no ordinary alien. This was a roots alien.

We walk up the gully, lead the alien to our shack, and introduce ourselves. The alien had a funny name that we couldn't say too good, so we decide to call it Maggy.

I said to Maggy, "Everybody on your planet look like you?"

"As a matter of fact, and that's quite intuitive, we do," said Maggy.

"You mean the same, down to yu toenail?"

"The same."

A cold chill go through me body and I begin to tremble when I really think about a whole planet that look like him. Maggy could see that I was worried.

"I know I look awful, but that's why I'm here. We don't like it either, so I've come for the antidote. But don't worry," Maggy said, "my condition is not contagious."

I breathe a sigh of relief.

So I decide to ask Maggy, "If you all look the same, how you tell the male from the female?"

"My dear boy," Maggy said, "haven't you figured that out yet?"

"Watch the boy business," said Uncle Obadiah. "Is me nephew, show some respect."

"Just some man-to-man humour to ease the tension," said Maggy. "I never really meant any harm," and then him went on to explain how him planet fall into such a state.

"After millions of years of in-breeding, our people were dying out from all sorts of genetic defects. We've been studying your planet for centuries, and when we realised that our bodies were almost like yours, we decided to introduce genes from your planet to our planet. The last time I was here, I collected thousands of gene samples from all over the Earth, but unfortunately, I crashed when I got back to my planet."

"Yu always crashing like this?" I asked.

"I always get what you would call 'bad vibes' when I enter your solar system. With all the wars, starvation, murder and suicide in your part of the universe, I've always found it necessary to stop off at a bar just outside your galaxy to order an Arcturus Assassin. It helps to settle my nerves."

This alien, I was beginning to figure out, besides being a great scientist, was an intergalactic drunk driver, and Uncle Obadiah said maybe we should put a big learner L on him spaceship so that other aliens would know to stay out of him way.

"Only one sample survived from the crash, and it belonged to the sweetest, kindest, gentlest person I met on the Earth. She was a young girl when I met her, but when she discovered I was from another planet, I had to erase all memory of myself from her mind with a new drug. It was premature, and no one knew how it would affect humans. We did know, however, that an overdose could have serious side effects. It could reverse positive character traits, and it could even kill certain key brain cells. But I had to do it. I gave her the drug and then made the fatal mistake of taking the cell samples after she got the drug."

"No wonder that woman so hard!" Uncle Obadiah shouted, "alien mind-drug warp her mind."

"I should look her up, to see how she's doing," suggested Maggy.

"Let sleeping dogs lie," said Uncle Obadiah. "We can never undo the past."

"The sample mixed with the drug saved our people, but produced this horrible side effect. It changed everyone's metabolism and now everyone looks like the woman you call Margaret Thatcher. I've come to Earth for the antidote. But again I gave into my single vice. I stopped off at the bar for another Arcturus Assassin and crashed again."

"So why you call I Menelik?" asked Uncle Obadiah.

"On the same visit to Earth, I collected cell samples from the man who was the ruler of the earth. He was a short man, with a trimmed beard and he wore a ring with two triangles -- the seal of royalty throughout the universe."

"Selassie I!" roared Uncle Obadiah.

"Precisely," said Maggy. "And you, Sir, bear a striking resemblance to his father."

"Maggy," said Uncle Obadiah, "yu soun like a real English man. Yu talk English good. For an alien."

Maggy blushed.

"So how yu get to know His Imperial Majesty?" asked Uncle Obadiah.

"Selassie," said Maggy "had the most superior genes of any one on Earth. He comes, as you may know, from a lineage of a family possessing all the characteristics of what we, as a specie, would have desired to resemble. Instead we are a freakish scientific mutation who look like a German frau who has eaten too many sour limes."

"Doan be so hard on yuself," said Uncle Obadiah. "Just give thanks you never take it from Queen Victoria."

Even Maggy who had traveled to the ends of the universe and back, and had seen so much, was frightened at such a prospect. Obadiah was right. Fate, in all its complexity, was kind. Yet there was some things that still confused him.

"I'll never understand though, how the other nations of the Earth, just stood by and watched Ethiopia being destroyed."

"Is a shame, yes," said Uncle Obadiah.

"From as early as the turn of the century," Maggy said, "we have been watching over Ethiopian affairs. With His Majesty's permission we intervened in the war between Ethiopia and Italy."

That explained it. For how else could a small rag-tag, ill-equipped army have defeated the great war machine of Europe without intergalactic help?

"For each shot an Ethiopian fired," Maggy continued, and pulled his laser gun from its holster, "I fired a laser from my spaceship and killed ten people. No one really knew the

11

difference for I was cloaked invisibly behind the clouds. In the end, it looked as if the Ethiopians had done it all alone, but the Ethiopians and Selassie himself knew they had received help from the heavens."

"So wha happen to His Majesty now?" probed Uncle Obadiah.

"Oh, he's fine. He's the king of our planet. That's why I'm here."

"Jah lives!" said Uncle Obadiah and him danced around the room, "Selassie I lives!"

"So what about all them news report dat His Majesty dead?" I asked.

"Don't believe anything that those newspapers and televisions tell you," said Maggy. "It's all a bunch of lies. The same people in Rome who opposed him on Earth, now oppose him even after his supposed death. I took His Majesty away during the last months of the coup," said Maggy with a touch of pride, "and substituted a clone of Selassie."

This explained to me why the army said His Imperial Majesty was behaving like a tyrant.

" It wasn't the real King of Kings," said Maggy, "just a lump of protoplasm engineered to look like His Imperial Majesty," and he put the laser gun back in its holster.

"No one ever killed His Majesty. He went with me back to my planet, and we accepted him as our king. There he rules justly and benevolently. We tried to change the results of the experiments, but nothing worked. Then His Majesty, in royal wisdom, decreed that I should go to Earth for the antidote, That's why I tried to land in your marijuana field. Throughout the universe, in all the galaxies, marijuana is used for a myriad of ailments. We know of its many uses, but never figured it could be used to reverse genetic defects. But as His Imperial Majesty said, 'Herb is for the healing of a nation'."

Well, from what Maggy said it seems as if Uncle Obadiah's herb could heal the universe.

Now Uncle Obadiah wasn't a drug dealer or anything like that. Him only grow enough for himself and the idren in the village. The police know about it, but them know Uncle Obadiah's herb was for meditation and reasoning, not for getting high like those American tourists do.

"I'd planned to snip a few buds from your crop, but took the last sip of the drink, lost control and landed in your field. I know I shouldn't be drinking the stuff, for His Majesty said that if I wanted to get high, then I should meditate on Jah."

Just as I was about to ask him if His Majesty and Jah was not the same, Uncle Obadiah uproot a whole plant and pop a spliff in Maggy's mouth.

"Try dis instead of yu Arcturus Assassin. Dis is de Jamaican Jamboree. An it won't give yu no headache or mek yu crash yu spaceship."

Maggy took a draw on the spliff and inhaled. And that was when the bangarang start.

Him head start to grow and him whole body start to shine. Him jump on Uncle Obadiah jackass and start ride through the countryside. All through Struie, Rat Trap, Lamb's River and Bethel Town. As him was riding the jackass, it look like him head disappear and that is why people down to this day still believe stories about rolling calves, duppies and headless horseman. All because of Maggy and Uncle Obadiah jackass.

We couldn't calm him down. And then it get worse. Him take out him laser gun and start fire it all over the place. At first it was great, for it was just disintegrating everything. We never mind. In fact, me think Uncle Obadiah wanted a stray shot to clap the busha up the hill for him grandfather was a slave owner in the old days, and him son was now a politician. But then Maggy fire a shot and disintegrate Uncle Obadiah's statue of Selassie.

That's when Uncle Obadiah wrath, and Maggy sober up same time. You never want to see a Rastaman wrath. Uncle Obadiah tell him right straight that him had to leave.

"Maggy, get off me land, get out of me village, get off me island. In fact, get off me planet. Leave Earth."

Maggy tried to apologize, but Uncle Obadiah wouldn't hear none of it. Uncle Obadiah just keep staring off into space, where him statue was, tarpaulin and all.

Maggy gather the samples and put them in him spaceship. Him tell me there had been a systemic failure in him navigational apparatus. Him never know where the hell him was.

"What was that stuff?" Maggy asked me.

"Lamb's breath," I said.

"I'd better dilute it to a thousandth of its strength. This is the best marijuana in this galaxy."

"We know," I said. "So please, sah, don't start running around and tell everybody in the universe. Make it be our secret. For if you tell everybody, then soon soon we going have spaceship landing in we backyard, blowing their horn, and pulling up to Uncle Obadiah's shack at all kinds of hours in the night, trying to buy herb that not for sale. Besides, me an Uncle Obadiah is the kind of people who like to keep to weself."

"It will be our secret," him said with a smile.

Then him apologize to Uncle Obadiah and said him could rebuild a duplicate from him spaceship.

"What done, done," said Uncle Obadiah and him accept Maggy apology for everything.

"So when yu coming back?" I ask Maggy.

"Selassie has decreed, " said Maggy, "that no one should return until all Africans have been reunited and all nations of the Earth accept His Imperial Majesty as its rightful ruler."

I wave good-bye because I know me wouldn't see him again.

"Jah guide," said Uncle Obadiah.

"Selassie lives," shouted Maggy from inside the spaceship, and blasted out of the universe, off course, but far away from Earth with antidote in tow.

I don't believe him did keep our field a secret though. For on some nights after Uncle Obadiah and me finish reasoning and smoking some herb, I see strange lights and all sort of things down in the gully. That's why Uncle Obadiah say if any alien come up to you house and ask you where Struie is, just point them north and as far away from him shack as possible, for him don't want Maggy coming over to him house, smoking all him herb, and shooting up the place with laser gun anymore.

SOFTERS
For Phyllis Washington

Everybody in Struie say me soft. I guess is because from when I was small I used to daydream, and when I fall asleep is a hard sleep. But the other reason is my two friend Ralph and Dicko. They was two of the roughest boys in the district. Ralph and Dicko never get sick, never break a arm or leg or never need stitches. Me, I would be out in the road with them and a teaspoon of rain would fall and I would catch a cold so bad my chest would sound like a patty-pan bus rumbling down the marl road. I would be sick as a dog in bed and would listen to them, for they was so loud, playing and fighting on the corner beside my uncle bar. They used to call we Trinity, but now is only me one: Dicko was the roughest, Ralph the toughest, and I was the softest. And they been dogging me from when I was a youth.

Even when I was in high school – and some mornings I used to lie in bed and watch the clouds coming over the myrtle grove, and end up late for school – I would hear them coming up the road. Instead of going through the front door of the house beside the bar, I would dress myself quick quick inside my uncle room and slip through the trap door near the closet. My uncle build the trap door before him operation for cancer so him wouldn't wake me and my mother late at night when him did have to go to the latrine. So I would slip down the trap door, run by the water tank beside the bar and come out near my little garden that I had near the bakery. The little garden never help my situation either. Besides calling me Softers,

16

Dicko used to call me Pumpkin Head, depending on him mood, which used to change faster than him spit could dry on the marl road.

Nobody but me and me uncle know about the trap door and plenty time I escape the two of them on the way to school. For if they did catch me, especially after me uncle give me a haircut, they would be fighting between themselves to see who would be the first to smash me neck. They would run after me and say, "Gentle Jesus meek and mild, Lord have mercy on this baldhead child," and smash me on me neck.

Usually Dicko won the race to get me, for he was the fastest and could usually outrun Ralph even when Ralph saw me first. The two of them was always in competition and I was the reserve or the umpire. We would have our Olympics to see who was the fastest, the strongest, or could jump the furthest. We would run all the way to Bethel Town and Dicko would drag me along until the last three-quarter mile and then take off, leaving me behind to see if Ralph walked any part of the way. He didn't care if I walked, I would come last anyway. He just wanted to tease. Ralph that he was softer than me, and so Ralph would run all the way to prove he wasn't soft like me. Dicko never trusted me though. When I told him Ralph wasn't walking, he always said that I took Ralph's side. But it wasn't true. I didn't like either of them. But if it came down to a choice of who would smash me, I would prefer Ralph because he didn't smash as hard. Everybody in Struie think that we is the best of friends. The truth was we wasn't friends, we just know each other for a long time. We went to primary school, then high school, and after my uncle dead from cancer a year ago and my mother went to Canada, we all stayed in the district. It was like I would never escape the two of them even though we was now big people.

Since I inherit the bar from my uncle, every Friday Dicko drive him jeep right up to the front of the bar where they use to tie up the horse and sit down in my uncle chair which him say was him favourite chair. Then Ralph show up, and they begin the evening with a game of skittles, arm wrestling, which I would have to judge, and a game of cut-throat dominoes which they would drag me into only because it was harder to read each other hand with me in the game. They would end the night trying to drink each other under the table.

Friday night was supposed to be my best night, after everybody was tired with the work in the fields, but I couldn't make a cent. The two of them was driving me to the poorhouse, frightening away my customers. Whenever Dicko get drunk, him take out him gun and start wave it around saying, "I going shoot, I going shoot the man who I know been poking my woman." Then Ralph would start to cry because him would remember a girl back in Mo Bay. "You know, you know, Pumpkin Head," he would say, "she was the only woman I ever love in me life, you know that. You know that, Pumpkin Head." And I would say, "Yes, yes, I know, I know," even though I never see her and the only time I see Dicko woman is when she flash by here in her jeep going down the road.

What was even worse than frightening my customers was they wouldn't pay me for the white rum they take off me shelf. And is not like they couldn't afford it. Dicko father own plenty hotel in Mo Bay and Dicko was in charge of a small hotel in Negril. Ralph father, who is the M.P. for the area, own a whole heap of car part store in Kingston and Mo Bay, and even though Ralph business was in Mo Bay, he would be at my bar every week. Ralph father and Ralph father father was the M. P. for the area. The family been in government since Queen Victoria was a virgin.

The two of them father run this district. Neither the police nor the law can touch them. The last policeman who try to lock up Dicko for resisting arrest, obscene language and disorderly conduct, get the beating of him life and then Dicko father get the policeman fired from the force. I never want to ask them for money either because I remember the last time in high school

I try to stand up to them and them turn on me. Dicko chase me with a dead bull frog and him say him was going make me eat it because I was too damn facety. I never run so fast in my life. That day, not even Dicko could catch me.

So every Friday the two of them inside my bar cursing, telling the same old story, and drinking my white rum without even offering me one. Ralph was bawling because he lose the only woman he ever loved and Dicko because he was afraid he would lose his woman. Between the two of them, I was losing the only business I ever had.

One time I said to Dicko, "But Dicko, what about all them woman you poking in Negril?" and he said to me, "First, not that is any of your fucking business who I poking, but I going tell you anyway. Darlene is my woman. She is mine. We have a pickney to show it. Flesh and blood. Anybody who want come between me and she going have to pay the same way, flesh and blood. Is just the principle. Just the principle."

That's when I ask him about the principle of paying me for the white rum and the two of them take it like an insult. Then Ralph laugh and say he would give me labour and parts free on my car whenever I get one. How me going get a car when them drinking off all my profit and the government taxing me on profit that I not making? And Dicko was just as bad. Him say I could spend as much time at him hotel as I want. But every time I go there, even the last time I get there, him tell me him full up. So I had to take the bus, without even a dinner mint from the restaurant, with my cardboard suitcase in me hand, back to Struie. I was lucky him never beat me on top of it.

Then six months ago Dicko get worse. Him was firing the gun in the air and saying, "I going kill the boy, kill the boy who been poking my woman. But first I going cut off him balls and give him for supper. Yeah, for supper. Curried balls for supper."

Then he pointed the gun and at me and said, "Touch it, touch it, Softers. You think I wouldn't do it." I wouldn't touch the gun, for nobody ever accuse me of being brave. So he just walked over to me and said, "You so soft, you little pumpkin head," and then smashed me on my neck the same way he been doing it now for twenty-five years. He ordered another white rum and get so drunk he couldn't move. Ralph was already passed out in a corner of the bar near the jukebox. I tried to get Dicko in the jeep myself, but I couldn't, for him was too heavy. So I send word down the road, by one on the minibuses that pass by here on the way to Rat Trap, for the boys on the farm to get him.

Thirty minutes go by without anybody, and then him girlfriend come to the bar. It was the first time I see her without dark glasses and hat, for she was always out 'shopping' as Dicko used to say. Well, the minute I see her I know why Dick was guarding this girl so. She had a body to dead for, and I was dead.

While we was cleaning him up, we start to talk. We talk about the new telephone line them was running down to Rat Trap and the new police station in Bethel Town, but we really hit it off when she tell me about the snails in her garden.

"I don't want to use any chemical on the tomatoes" she said. "It might harm my little girl. I want her to get fresh vegetables, but I don't want anything to happen to her later in life; it might poison her, you know. She is the only thing in this life I have."

I said to her, "All you have to do is put some beer inside paper cup and the snail will crawl inside and drown. I don't know if is the smell of the beer that drive them wild, but it always work for me."

So we cleaned up Dicko and loaded him into the back of the jeep, and the next day I delivered a case of beer, personally, to her house. She told me not to come back to the house because it was dangerous, but two weeks later she came up to the bar and give me a juicy, red tomato, fresh from her garden. That day we talked for three hours before she went shopping. From then on, we begin to share garden secrets, and that was how the business start.

Dicko would leave for the hotel on Monday and she would go shopping as usual, even if she didn't have any money, everyday till Friday when him come back. On the way back from Mo Bay, she would park her jeep behind the bakery so nobody could see it from the road, and we would talk until it was time for her to go home. Sometimes the two of we would fall asleep, and I would have to slip her out through the trap door in my uncle room.

This was going on for three months without Dicko knowing anything. Him was still coming to the bar and getting drunk while Ralph would stare at me like I owe him money. Some nights I used to say to her, "If I was a man, if I wasn't so soft, I would walk down to the hotel and tell him about the two of we."

She said, "Then you would be a dead man. You is the only man I want in me bed. And let me tell you, you soft for the right things and hard for the rest." I tell you that girl know how to put starch in my pants.

So I ask her, "So if things so bad, why you don't leave him?"

"Because," she said, "Dicko say if I ever try to leave, I would never see my little girl again. Him say him would kill me before him would see me with another man."

And that's when she would cry and all I could do was rub her arm and shoulder and she would fall asleep on my lap. That's when I used to think whether I really did love her, if it was pity, or if it was because we both hated Dicko so much. She was getting her revenge by spending every cent of her allowance. But was I getting revenge by sleeping with his woman? It didn't feel that way. Sometimes we would lay in bed and dream of how we would pick up and go live with her aunt in Darliston, but then she would remember her little girl, Olive, and we would change the subject. Then we would wait through the weekend without seeing each other until Dicko would leave for Negril.

Then, one night, Darlene sneaked out of the house after

21

Dicko left the bar and look like he finally passed out on the sofa at their house, and come to the bar to see me. She park the jeep right in front of the bar and run inside.

When I see her I said, "You mad, girl. What you doing here? You going get the two of we dead!"

Then she show me her bruises and said, "I don't care no more! Make him kill me. Him can kill me now. This is first time in my whole wretched life I ever feel so happy, so I can dead now. I ready!"

And I couldn't say a thing, for I did feel the same way. I close up the bar and left Ralph sleeping in the corner and we go back to my room.

At about three o'clock in the morning, I wake up to, "Boof, boof, boof, boof boof, boof," on the bar door. It was Dicko. She never know that Dicko was following her. Me and Darlene catch afraid. We never know what to do. I say to her, "Run down to me uncle room and slip out as you usually do," and she said, "But him will kill you," and I said, "If him going kill anybody, make him kill me. You have to think about Olive." When she hear that, she kiss me and slip through the trap door.

I go to the front door and I call to Dicko and him come running around to the front door and say, "I going kill the boy, I going kill the boy who been poking my woman."

And I brace myself by the door, all now I don't know where I get the courage to say to him, "Yes, yes is me. I been poking your woman. Shoot me right here."

And, as drunk as him was, him laugh and say, "Get out of my way, you little raas. It could never be you. You with my woman! You too fucking soft for a woman like that. You wouldn't know what to do with her. Is that raas Ralph I looking for, and now I catch him after all these years."

As he run past me, he saw Darlene near the water tank. "See, see, you see her," he said. "I always know you was taking his side. But to lose you life for him, you mad or something, boy?" and him smashed me on my neck.

Him grab my hand and say, "You going help me, help me find that boy who been poking my woman," and we run out though the front door into the darkness. I was there grinning, without letting him see me, thinking that it was me and Dicko out in the copse looking for me!

Him fire a shot in the air and that wake up Ralph. Then Dicko shout, "You better come out now, Ralph. Take the bullet easy. Don't make me have to track you down. You is me friend. I promise you it will only be one bullet."

When Ralph hear that, he burst through the bar door and see Darlene starting up the jeep. Him jump inside the back of the jeep, and Darlene help him to get in.

And just by the way she hold him, just by the way she help him get in the jeep, I know she had the two of we, me and Dicko, soft.

Dicko fire a shot at the jeep, but him was too drunk to shoot straight, and him shoot off the Red Stripe sign off the corner of the bar. Darlene and Ralph disappear in the darkness on the road to Bethel Town.

When Dicko see the tail-lights going around the corner, him start to scream,

"You little raas, you little raas, I always know it was you," and him throw down the gun in the middle of the road.

I hold him up and him said, "I always know it was that little fucker. One of the boys see him with her down by the bakery last week, but I did want to catch the two of them so I could shoot them together." I pick up the gun for him and the two of we walk back to the bar and I put him in him my uncle chair. Then, for the first time in him life, him pay me for a bottle of white rum and invite me for a drink.

"And you know," he said, "is not because of any great love affair why I would shoot the boy, is just the principle, just the principle," and passed out. I put the cap on the bottle, put the bottle back on the shelf, and left him there until morning to sleep it off.

A week later Darlene came back to Struie because Dicko was going throw Olive out on the street with nothing. "I don't even know if is my pickney him say, and him take away everything from Darlene: clothes, jewellery, and the jeep. Him say him don't want nothing to do with them no more, and leave Darlene and Olive with the clothes on them back and two scandal bags of shoes and underwear.

I was cleaning up the bar when Darlene come inside with Olive. She order a beer for herself and a kola champagne for Olive. She walk over to the window and I give her the Red Stripe in a bottle and serve Olive in a glass. The two of them sit down quiet quiet looking through the window, and I never say nothing to her. She drink the beer, and she wait for Olive to finish the soft drink. Then she get up to open her purse to pay me.

I say, "Don't worry, everything is on me, like it always is."

She never say nothing but close the purse and tell Olive to wipe her mouth and she pick up the bags. The two of them walk through the door and head down by Soldier's Tomb so they could catch a minibus going to Darliston.

I was picking up the bottles when she come back inside the bar with the two bag in her hand and say, "I never mean to hurt you. I never really mean to. I only did it to protect you."

"Protect me! Protect me!" I said. "You poking another man to protect me. Girl, you gone mad now!"

She said, "You don't understand. Ralph catch me one night when I was leaving here, and him say if I never give him sex, him would tell Dicko about me and you. So I give him."

"For how long?" I ask.

"Four month," she say.

"So all that time when you in my bed, you couldn't wait to get downstairs to meet up with Ralph, eh."

"Is not like that. Is not like that at all. Nearly every time I leave here, is him was waiting for me. Is him was following me. And I couldn't just have sex and leave. I not like that. So I start to tell him about me and you and then I get confuse."

"Confuse. Confuse. You married to one man, sleeping with me, and telling another man about me and you while him poking you and you say you confuse. You mad!"

"I wasn't sure," she said, "if you was in love with me or you was just using me."

"You wasn't sure, so you go on and have sex with another man who would really use you, to be sure, and on top of it talking to him about me. How you think that make me feel? Get out, get out of the bar right now! Right now! Get out!"

She turn her back to me and she walk out to the front of the bar. Olive was picking flowers down by the roadside.

"All them lies," I said, "all the them lies you tell me. I was a real jackass to believe you. All them lies about how you love me."

"I never tell you a lie in my life," she said. "Never."

"See, see, more lies," I said. "Girl where you get the nerve?"

"Believe what you want to believe," she said. "I gone." And she step off the front of the bar down into the road. "But remember," she said, "I never lie to you."

A minibus was easing up the road and was swaying from side to side the way it was packed. Olive put the flowers in her hair and started flagging down the bus.

Darlene picked up the bags with their clothes and slung it over her back.

"How I to believe you?" I ask.

She walk past me and went inside the bar. She put the bags on the counter, open a bottle of Red Stripe and pour half of it into a paper cup. She give me the bottle and she drink out of the paper cup.

"What this mean?" I ask her.

"Think about it," she said and she drink down all the beer, then run down the road to catch the minibus that was already getting ready to leave her. The minibus belch a cloud of black smoke and Olive waved to me as it turned around the corner.

Two months go by and Ralph never come back to Struie.

Dicko say if him ever see Ralph in Struie, him would shoot him on sight, no questions asked. And the only time I see Dicko is when him drive by the bar on the way to him house.

Things really quiet around here, and all my customers back at the bar. I really didn't know what to believe anymore, but last month, I take a minibus to Darliston to get Olive and Darlene. I really did miss her. Olive sleeping inside my uncle room, and the bar finally making money. I know that when the men come inside here, by the way they look at me, I know them laughing at me behind them back. And I know what they calling me. But make them laugh at me. Make them laugh at me for having a woman that no man in the district want because everybody know about her now. All I know is that late at night, when me and Darlene hug up tight tight inside my bed, and she is with me, and me alone, I feel like the biggest man in the world. So make them, make them call me, Softers.

CURLY LOCKS

The urgent throb of Family Man's bass tumbled over the blades of grass and rattled the aluminium jalousies of my room. Opening the window, I saw Ras Emmanuel standing under his Bombay mango tree watering the rows of tomato seedlings he had planted that summer. Ras Emmanuel had really cleaned up the place. He had inherited the house from his grandfather, but the property had been tied up in probate court because his grandfather had died without leaving a will.

The house lay abandoned for two years, surrounded by weeds and vines before Ras Emmanuel moved in and began planting his gardens with fruit trees and vegetables.

"Hail Ras-Emmanuel," I said. He waved to me and pointed with pride to a banner announcing the One Love Concert at the National Stadium where Bob Marley was going to perform. I had worked on the banner with Ras Emmanuel. He was an elder in the Twelve Tribes of Israel and a friend of Bob, and he had been showing the banner to the brethren. I had designed the banner from an early picture of Bob. At that time it was hard to tell whether Bob had dreadlocks or if his hair was just long like mine, but I used that picture because of the fierceness in his eyes. Ras Emmanuel had even shown the banner to Bob and I was interested in hearing what he had to say about it.

It was a day before the concert that Ras Emmanuel had said to me, "I guwane down by Island House tonight. I guwane show Bob the banner," and Pamela, my queen, was so excited she couldn't let go of my arm and neck all night while we were hanging out at Kreamy Corner. It felt so good standing out there on Hope Road with her by my side, Congo rude boy and uptown queen.

I was wearing my red, green and gold tam, Natty Dread T-shirt, blue jeans and Adidas sneakers. And there she was, my queen, in a gold tam, red, green and gold tie-dye T-shirt, and a long green skirt that covered her ankles. All the dreads passed by and bowed their heads, while I just kotch cool, cool.

We weren't afraid of anyone – not the neighbours with their su-su, not even her father, Dr. McKenzie, who when he found us kissing outside the gate that night, ordered her inside.

"Get inside, young lady," he said. It was the first time I ever heard him raise his voice at her. "And you, Sir, I thought would know how to treat a young lady, but apparently you don't," he snapped, and then escorted her inside. I was going to answer him, but Pamela put her fingers over her lips and motioned to me to keep quiet.

I was so mad I couldn't sleep. It was about five o'clock when I finally fell asleep and couldn't wake up until about ten o'clock, long after my Aunt Dorothy and Uncle Raymond had left for their usual Saturday visit to the civil service club.

I didn't expect them to be home until at least four o'clock. I ran through the front door and through the carport and checked the padlock on the wrought iron security gates my Aunt Dorothy had just installed at the back door of the kitchen.

The concrete hadn't dried yet, and I didn't want to get in trouble that particular day.

The gate had been put in because my Aunt Dorothy had gone berserk after she was held up by two young rascals (my Uncle Raymond says Rastas, but he doesn't know any better) in the driveway of our house. The workmen came and built concrete fences at the side of the house, with broken beer bottles planted on the top to prevent anyone, including me, from climbing over the fence. Now I had to take the long way to get to Ras Emmanuel's house.

Uncle Raymond had supervised the entire job, walking around the men, glass of Johnny Walker in hand, chupsing and finding fault with nearly everything the men did. He was always like that. I could never tell where he was – it was like he had eyes everywhere. And he was on the watch even more because he didn't like the fact that one of the workmen was a young Rasta.

"All those Rastas should be rounded up," said Uncle Raymond later that night, as he sat on the verandah and mixed himself a screwdriver.

"For once I agree with you Uncle Raymond," I said.

"You do?" he said.

"Yes, I do. Round them all up and send them back to Ethiopia. That's all they're asking for. They want to return to the fatherland."

That didn't go down too well with him at all. And the problem was that I'd said it when Dr. McKenzie, principal of St. Brendon's Boys' School, was there. Three weeks before, he had expelled two boys for refusing to cut off their dreadlocks, and chanting, "Blood, blood, blood and fiah for the Pope, the Pope of Rome," right in the middle of the *Tantum Ergo*. I probably should have kept my mouth shut and not defended the brethren, but like Ras Emmanuel always says, "Whoever confess His Majesty before men and people, His Majesty will confess him in heaven."

After I said that, Uncle Raymond dismissed me, as he usually did, with a flick of his fingers. I was banished once again from his sight which was okay with me. I hated to be under his roof, for despite all appearances of his being the ultimate family man, he used to beat Aunt Dorothy, and for no reason whatsoever. His shirt not ironed right. BIFF. The creases in his pants not straight. BAFF. His socks not laid out with his pants. BOOF. Shoes not cleaned. BOOF, BOOF, BOOF. Aunt Dorothy had fallen again.

And the worst part was I couldn't do a thing. Besides the fact that he was much bigger than me – he probably would have liked me to take a swing at him, so he could beat me to death – Aunt Dorothy begged me not to do anything.

"One good one, Aunt Dorothy, that's all I want to do, one good blow and then he can kill me," I said.

But she told me not to do anything. She said everything was her fault, and that I shouldn't do anything until my mother sent for me from the States.

But that was taking too long. I'd been with them now for two years since my mother, a poor high-school teacher who worked in Franklin Town, couldn't take life in Jamaica anymore and decided to move to Miami. I had tried to get a visa, but I had been turned down for a visitor's visa several times because according to them, I had no reason to return to the island. So she applied and they had given her a visa without hesitation. Everything was irie. She owned her own home, she had never divorced my father (although no one knew where he was) and she had stable employment. She got her visitor's visa, went to Miami and since then she'd been working as a maid in the Diplomat Hotel in order to prove she could take care of me when she filed for me. But I was in no hurry to leave Jamaica.

During this time, my mother sold our house to Uncle Raymond with the promise that he'd use some of his connections in the States to change Jamaican dollars into American dollars. He was now a member of the middle class. He had a Mona house, a loyal wife, and a daughter in college in America. He was now living alongside doctors, lawyers and professors from U.W.I. – all the kind of people he wanted to associate with since he joined the civil service as a lowly customs clerk and climbed all the way, I must admit it, through hard work, to the post of chief financial officer in customs. So it used to burn me, really, to see him sucking up to Pamela's father, Dr. McKenzie, who had just moved in on our block. A real Jamaican brown man, Dr. McKenzie was short, round-faced, and baldheaded. He belonged to one of the richest families in the island, but was regarded as a bit of an eccentric because, despite the family's wealth, he had gone to Britain, studied at Oxford, and had excelled in English, a fact he would never let us forget. The minute he moved onto our block, Uncle Raymond invited him over for drinks. That a man who came from such wealth could turn his back on all that money in his family and could now only afford to move in beside someone like him was something Uncle Raymond wanted to explore further.

Dr. McKenzie had moved from St. Catherine to Mona when our former neighbours, the Clarkes, moved back to England. Mr. Clarke got frightened when he heard the words "socialism" and "black power" and left Jamaica immediately. He told his good friend from Oxford, Dr. McKenzie, about his plans and the two of them came to a gentleman's agreement over the price. It didn't matter to me whether or not the Clarkes stayed or left, but when Dr. McKenzie moved in, it did matter.

And for one reason only. I met Pamela.

Pamela was a curious mixture. She was Dr. McKenzie's only child from a brief marriage. The rumour was that Mrs. McKenzie, a white woman from Kent, never thought there would be so many black people in Jamaica, and she was very uncomfortable being around so many black people. She thought everyone in Jamaica looked like Dr. McKenzie. After two years, she gave him an ultimatum, either he came back to England with her or she would leave him. He stayed.

Pamela was taller than her father, and had slightly broad hips and slender legs, which were usually concealed by the starched white uniforms she wore to school.

She had brown eyes and mocha-brown skin – a shade lighter than Judy Mowatt of the I-Threes – and short black hair which curled naturally into braids and framed her face. She was my little curly locks.

Dr. McKenzie was very proud of Pamela. I could tell exactly when he was going to say something about her. His voice

31

changed, became softer, almost like how she sounded when she talked about him. That man, you could tell by his tone, wouldn't let breeze blow hard against his daughter. It was not the same tone he used when he talked about me. I had barely squeezed through to sixth form, was on the verge of failing all my "A" levels, except art, and I was now associating with Rastas.

He often reminded me that she came from good family and had gone to all the right schools, including Immaculate Conception. Clearly I was on the road to becoming a wastrel, and he didn't want Pamela with someone like me.

We had studied together for our "A" levels and we were both reading the same books for English literature. We would have these long discussions about Dickens, Joyce, Forster, and then we would eventually come back to our favourite topics, the classic authors of West Indian literature, Lamming, Brathwaite, Walcott.

Everyone was surprised, even me, that she was my queen. Dr. McKenzie ignored us, and he pretended nothing was happening.

Uncle Raymond was even more confused. He couldn't understand how a girl like her, good-looking, brown-skinned, and a lot smarter than me, could even dream of being seen with me. But I knew better. The girl was roots.

In fact, it was hard to tell who loved Bob's music more, me or her. I loved to see her in the long, flowing skirts, (she looked like one of the sistren) and we would go over to Ras Emmanuel's house. We'd sit there for hours and listen to the old songs by Bob like "Lonesome Feelings," and "It Hurts to be Alone." Sometimes Ras Emmanuel had bootleg copies of songs Bob had done in the studio, some of which were to be released in the future, and some which have never been released. She'd read most of the books in her father's library, and it was she who taught me that Bob was a shaman, and a prophet – a hero by the fact of the mystery surrounding his birth, his exile in America and now his return to Jamaica to sing redemption songs in the National Stadium. Jah, I loved this daughter – she was even more roots than me. She was the one who talked me into getting the tickets for the One Love Concert.

She had never been to a Bob Marley concert before and neither had I. I hadn't been able to go to the first two concerts he did with Michael Jackson or Stevie Wonder because my mother wouldn't give me the money. She said it was too dangerous. In some ways my mother, Dr. McKenzie, Aunt Dorothy and Uncle Raymond are all alike. They all grew up in a time when Rastas were seen by the British, who still ruled Jamaica at that time, as threats to society, and they *were* a threat to British Babylonian society.

They saw Rastas as herb-smoking, violent men who breeded randomly and wantonly, and who had taken to the hills in the east to live in communes. But youth like me, who grew up in freer times, who understood the brethren, knew that we had to give up all of that middle-class madness. It was all One Love, One Aim, One Destiny.

But people like Dr. McKenzie, Aunt Dorothy and Uncle Raymond couldn't see beyond shade of skin – my aunt, a black woman, tried to *Ponds* away her blackness. When I said this to Pam, she said I was sounding more Rasta every day, which sounded like an insult the way she said it, but I let it pass for she was my queen.

As I opened the gate to Pamela's house (I usually jumped over the top, but today I didn't want to get her father angry), I saw Pamela by the door with her father.

She was wearing a pink and white outfit her mother had sent for her. When she saw me, she felt a little uncomfortable because she knew how I felt about her wearing those kinds of clothes. The skirt was at least two inches above her knee. But I knew she was probably wearing it to please her father, so I didn't say anything.

"So are you excited?" I asked, slipping into my best imitation of the Queen's English, which I hated. For every syllable, every sound reminded me I was of a different colour and class, but I didn't want to give her father any reason for grounding her.

"There's something I want to tell you," she said.

"Don't worry about the bike," I said. "I borrowed the car from Uncle Raymond. I washed and cleaned it in exchange for borrowing it."

Dr. McKenzie wouldn't allow Pamela to ride on the back of my bike, so I had bribed my Uncle to borrow his car. I promised him I would clean the car for an entire month if I could borrow it for the night.

"I'll pick you up at five," I said.

"She'll be having a chat with you this afternoon," said Dr. McKenzie, interrupting us. And before she could say anything," he said. "Come along now, Pamela, we must be going."

Pamela got into the car with her father, and I closed the gate for them. She waved to me, but she had a worried look on her face, but I knew that I was probably because she thought I was still upset about the pink outfit.

I turned up the road and ran towards Ras Emmanuel's house. He was still watering his plants. The hose snaked around the roots of an ackee tree he had planted in the centre of his front yard.

"Ites, dread," I said.

"Rastafari," he said. " So de I ready fa tonight. De I and him queen reddy fe fawud."

"Yes, dread," I answered.

"Dere's only one problem yu have now," said Ras Emmanuel. "What?"

Ras Emmanuel placed the hose at the roots of the tree and turned it off. We walked around to the back of the house, and he pointed to my banner.

"I been showin dis off," he said.

"I know."

"All de idren love it," he said. "I show it to the whole band, and Bob own art man love it. Bob himself love it."

34

"Bob saw it and loved it!"

"Bob waan fe meet the I before the concert start."

"So what's the problem?" I asked.

Ras Emmanuel walked over to me and pulled the tam off my head.

"Bob rehearsin fa de concert tonight. We can go down to Island House, but dem naw go let yu in as a bald head, no matter how much hair yu have. Yu have to be a dreadlock."

"So why can't I wear my tam?"

"Since dem shoot him las year, him naw allow nobody inside the studio wid tam. Dem can have a gun inside the tam. Only dreadlocks inside the studio. Man to man. Dreadlock to dreadlock. Tonight him even going wear the ring that Selassie himself wear. The ring with the Lion of the tribe of Judah."

"No, you're making this up!"

"Is me mekkin' things up or you?"

I didn't understand what he meant by that, but I wanted to hear more about my chance to meet Bob.

"So what am I going to do?"

"Das why me call yu over here."

Ras Emmanuel led me to his living room. Inside his queen, Sister Joy, was sitting on the sofa. She was knitting a tam for Ras Emmanuel. I nodded to her and she nodded back. Ras Emmanuel put *Rastaman Vibration* on the turntable, and turned down the bass. He explained to me that Sister Joy and some of the other sistren had finished the locks on a girl from Beverly Hills who had bought at least six bottles of Sebastian Mud to make her dreadlocks. He said there was enough left over to do my hair, and it would dry in time for the concert.

"Yu cyaan wear de tam fa de res a de aftanoon," he said. "Dis is a serius ting. But yu haffi decide."

"I'm ready."

Ras Emmanuel looked surprised that I answered so quickly, but all that was in my mind was that I was going to meet Bob. I could always wash it out the next day, but I wouldn't let him know that.

I sat there inside Ras Emmanuel's bedroom and the sistren worked on my hair for five hours, on and off.

When I got up and looked at myself in the mirror, I could barely recognise myself. I was a dreadlocks. But what was strange was that it seemed so inevitable.

The feel of the locks on my shoulders, the change in the colour and the texture was unbelievable. The locks, as Ras Emmanuel called them – antenna to Jah – made me realise why Babylon and baldheads feared the Rastaman. A Rastaman's locks, like Samson's, gave him power over all creation. I felt in total control.

But now I had to figure out how I was going to get around without Uncle Raymond, Aunt Dorothy and Dr. McKenzie seeing me. I knew Pamela would understand.

When they were finished, it was almost three o'clock, barely enough time to shower and get dressed. I figured I could tell Pamela to meet me over at my house, then slip out before my Uncle Raymond came back home. But I had to time everything perfectly.

"Jah guide," said Ras Emmanuel as I left his house. "An remember, I and I is next door if de I need anyting."

When I got home, I took a shower, and changed into a T-shirt Ras Emmanuel had given me with the Solomonic seal on the front in red, green and gold. I had just finished dressing when I heard the familiar cough of Aunt Dorothy's car. I called Pamela on the phone and told her to meet at the front of my house, but she said I should come over to her house. I couldn't slip out the back door, for they hadn't opened the padlock. So I had to wait until Uncle Raymond and Aunt Dorothy were inside the house before I slipped out.

"Herbert, are you here?" said my Aunt Dorothy.

"I'm here," I said.

"Come here quick," she said. "We have a surprise for you."

"I'll soon be there."

I waited until she was inside her room and then listened for them to settle into their usual patterns. I listened to the shuffle of Uncle Raymond's shoes. He always got drunk when he got together with his civil service friends. My aunt closed the door to her room to undress, and my uncle went to the kitchen to mix himself a drink.

This was my chance. As I slipped out the front door, I saw the surprise on the sofa. A brand new three-piece suit to wear to the concert.

I thought I had run out of the house without anyone seeing me, but as I jumped over the gate to Pamela's house, a hand dragged me down and pushed me to the ground. I screamed and the hand recoiled after it hit me.

"Herbert, Herbert, is that you like that?" said my Uncle Raymond.

The commotion brought Pamela and her father outside, and the minute she saw me, she said, "My God, Herbert, what have you done to your hair!"

"It will wash out," I said. "It's only for today, for the concert."

"You aren't going anywhere like that with my daughter!" said Dr. McKenzie.

"I knew this boy wouldn't turn out right. Wha cyaan come good a morning, cyaan come good a evening," said Uncle Raymond. "And you can forget about borrowing my car!"

"But you promised!"

"I made the promise to Herbert, NOT Rasta Herbert."

They had all turned on me. My Aunt Dorothy walked away without even saying a word.

I took Pamela by the hand and said to her, "Pamela, I did this for a reason."

"What reason could you have for doing this?" she asked.

"Bob, Pamela. I'm going to meet brother Bob. Bob Marley."

"And?"

"You don't want to come with me?"

"Herbert, I can't."

"Not even to see the King?"

"Not even to see the King. This is too much for me to handle. This is just too much for me." She touched me on my forearm and walked over to her father's side.

I crossed the road and walked over to my bike and started it. Uncle Raymond started screaming, "If you leave here, if you leave here looking like that, then you better not come back!"

I flashed my dreadlocks, got on my bike, and kick-started it. I looked through the window at my Aunt Dorothy and she was staring over the fence to Ras Emmanuel's house. She was shaking her head.

I turned the handle, looked at Pamela, and hoped she would change her mind, jump on the back of my bike, and ride with me down to Island House. She looked away. I throttled the bike, turned south, and raced the engine to meet the King.

THE DAY MRS. HO SANG GOT ARRESTED

We never really meant to get Mrs. Ho Sang in trouble, but that's the way it turned out. Nobody could have known that Corporal Ramsay hated her so much. Afterwards everybody said they saw it coming, but I don't believe them. Who would ever think that a God-fearing, Christian woman like Mrs. Ho Sang could ever end up in jail. Besides, everything is always clear after trouble start.

Nobody can know exactly how it began, but it was probably when Corporal Ramsay started calling her son, Bradford, 'The Angel of Destruction'. Corporal Ramsay never called Bradford 'The Angel of Destruction' to his face, but from the time he said it, all the other parents on the block started to call Bradford 'The Angel'. Mrs. Ho Sang never liked that, for if there were two things in this world that Mrs. Ho Sang loved, they were Bradford and her garden.

From the time I've known Bradford, he was always the best dressed boy on the block, and that was because of his mother. When all of us were outside, running about barefoot with our hair still uncombed, teeth barely brushed, and faces unwashed, Bradford, *if* his mother let him out, would always come out with every hair in place and always wearing sneakers. In fact, in the twenty years I've known him, I have never seen Bradford without shoes. His mother gave him everything he wanted. Even at Christmas, at the annual fair at the community centre, he always had at least thirty dollars to spend on the merry-go-round or Ferris wheel. That is why I think it hurt Mrs. Ho Sang so much when some took it a bit too far and called him, 'Gabriel'.

True, Bradford used to break at lot of things, but those were all accidents. He was really clumsy, and he broke a lot of toys that belonged to Kevin, Corporal Ramsay's only son. The toys didn't cost much money, it was just that Corporal Ramsay wanted to hang onto them. But whenever his mother visited Mrs. Ramsay and Bradford went along, for she couldn't leave him in the house alone, (everyone said she was secretly afraid he would burn the place down), he would break something that belonged to Kevin. One thing though, Bradford was an honest person. If he broke something, or did anything wrong, he never tried to conceal it.

He always told the truth. And I guess, that's another reason why his mother loved him so much. He never lied to her.

The name really stuck when one day we were playing cricket in the street. We had definite rules for street cricket, and most of them were like regular cricket, but the strictest rule was the six run rule and Mrs. Smith's house. If you hit the ball over her fence, you got six runs, but you were out.

Mrs. Smith was this old English lady who lived on the block from the time the Matalons first built houses in the area. When her daughter, Jennifer, died and Mrs. Smith had no one to take care of her and give her the proper dose of her medications, she became more and more senile and afraid of Rastas with their sombre faces and wild, untamed dreadlocks. She saw Rastas everywhere. Rastas behind her fence, Rastas in her mango tree, Rastas coming through the cracks in her door like cockroaches. So everyday she would sit by her kitchen door, armed with her hose and the gun nozzle on full blast, and sprayed anyone who came through the gates. Even the postman got wet one day, and from then on, he dropped her mail over the fence.

Nobody liked getting wet, for if you did you would have to explain to your parents how you got wet, and she would have called your parents already, so not only would you get wet, but you would also probably get a beating from your father for bothering the old lady. Plus, sometimes she took the ball away and never gave it back, no matter how much you pleaded. So that's why we invented the rule. Six runs over Mrs. Smith's house and you were out.

Well, one day right after summer holidays began, we were playing cricket and I bowled Bradford a bouncer that was sweet like a St. Julian Mango, and he couldn't resist it. Bradford loved hitting bouncers, and he knew the new girl that had just moved in on the block was watching us from her verandah. Bradford wanted to impress her, so they could have something to talk about after church on Sundays.

They went to different schools, but the same church. He went to St. George's All Boys and she went to Immaculate Conception. I never had a chance with her. I went to Kingston College and it was very Anglican. I was too black, and too Protestant.

So Bradford got on his back leg and hit the ball up in the air. That was what I wanted so I could get a chance to catch the ball, but I didn't think he wanted to hit the ball so hard. The ball sailed right over my head and into Mrs. Smith's yard. I just looked at him. That was the end of the match. I won, but it was only ten o'clock in the morning, and we didn't have a ball for the rest of the day, and probably the whole summer. Nobody even had a spare. I told Bradford he would have to go for the ball. I guess he wanted to show off how brave he was, so he puffed up his chest, marched over to the fence and jumped over.

Before his feet could touch the ground, Mrs. Smith came charging out of her kitchen door on her spindly little white legs and with the hose at full blast and wet Bradford from head to toe. With all her shrieking, everybody on the block came out to see Bradford still getting wet by Mrs. Smith. Even the new girl was laughing.

Bradford was so embarrassed. But he never said a word,

that's just how he was. It took him a long while for his temper to rise, but when it did, there was bound to be trouble. He just picked up the ball, threw it to me and jumped over the fence. And even then, Mrs. Smith was still wetting him.

The next morning she woke up like her house was on fire. They were thinking of admitting her to Bellevue. She had phoned the police several times, but they never responded because she was always calling about Rastas coming into her yard. But this time, she said it was different. She said a Rastaman had shot holes in her glass jalousies. They ignored her until she said she was going to call her son-in law who knew the commissioner and he was going to call the local Member of Parliament. The sergeant at the desk, rather than go through all of that hassle, called Corporal Ramsay and asked him to look in on her just before he came to work. Sure enough, when Corporal Ramsay got there, the panes had been shot through. But the panes had been damaged in what seemed to him a curious way. Every other pane in the window had been shot through. And the gunman had deliberately done this in every other window around her house. Mrs. Smith was sure it was a Rasta, but Corporal Ramsay ignored her. He reported the incident and decided to investigate.

He soon found out that the holes had been caused by a BB gun, and gathered as many pellets as he could find from inside Mrs. Smith's house. He then rounded up all the boys on the block, and he learned that Bradford was the only one who had a BB gun. When Corporal Ramsay confronted Bradford's father, Mr. Ho Sang said, "My son would never do that. Only a mad man would do something so purposeful, and I don't know anybody like that or have anybody like that in my family. I going to get you fired for this. You just watch and see. I going to get you fired for this!"

But when Corporal Ramsay produced all the facts, none of which proved anything, but just pointed the finger in Bradford's direction, Bradford confessed, "I did it. I did it, Daddy. It was me."

Corporal Ramsay used to laugh when he told people what happened next. He said it was the first time he saw a yellow man turn red. It was also the first time he called Bradford, 'The Angel of Destruction'. Mr. Ho Sang couldn't speak. What was even worse, they found the Rasta tam with red, gold and green, and the mop that Bradford had dyed black and used to cover his head. Mr. Ho Sang barely spoke to Bradford after that, but Mrs. Ho Sang never believed any of it. She said her son would never have done anything like that, and everyone was just jealous of her son and her wonderful garden.

And part of it was true: a lot of people *were* jealous of her garden. It was something to envy. All the flower beds were six feet by three feet by three feet deep, and had a variety of roses, petunias and begonias growing in each bed. She would measure and dig the beds herself. She would remove all the soil, and fill the hole with cow manure which she collected from a pasture behind the primary school we had all attended. Some evenings, you could see her coming home, wearing the big Chinese straw hat and a big crocus bag strapped over her shoulders, and her face freckled with cow manure.

After she was finished putting down all the manure, she would put in a six inch layer of peat moss, and soil she had brought down from the banks of the Hope River near Papine. Next she spread yard clippings from her plants and lawn. She would let it settle for a few weeks and then mulch the bed with potato, carrot, lettuce and bok choy peelings from her kitchen. The whole garden would then be surrounded by limestone rocks which she again would put in by hand, one by one, stone by stone.

It was one of these days when she was on her knees, edging along the fence, that she saw Corporal Ramsay carrying on with his maid. She pretended she hadn't seen anything, but all three of them knew what had happened, so Corporal Ramsay scurried off around the corner of his house and probably continued to do what he had been doing. This time out of Mrs. Ho Sang's sight.

From that day on, Corporal Ramsay walked around with his head hung low. Every time he saw Mrs. Ho Sang, he would barely whisper, "Good Morning" or "Good Afternoon." Mrs. Ho Sang, for her part, would never have said anything if one day, when they were playing their usual game of bridge at my mother's house, it had not slipped out, and Mrs. Ramsay called Bradford, 'Gabriel'.

Mrs. Ho Sang didn't show any emotion, but just said under her breath, "My son is not an angel, but the last time I saw your husband, he was helping the maid put out more than the laundry."

That was it. Mrs. Ramsay left the table, packed her bags and went to live with her mother in Edgewater. It was then everyone said Mr. Ramsay started to plot his revenge, for he blamed the breakup of his marriage on Mrs. Ho Sang.

He tried everything. He tried to enforce city ordinances, code violations, anything, but Mrs. Ho Sang was always in compliance. This was a woman who used to gather food for poor people! He couldn't lay a finger on her. So he figured, if you can't catch Quashie, you catch him shirt.

He arrested Mr. Ho Sang several times for drunk-driving, but Mrs. Ho Sang didn't care. She was tired of all his lies about working late when she knew he was spending his time with the go-go girls in the club that he had just bought. And Mr. Ho Sang was so drunk most of the time now that nothing mattered to him.

Corporal Ramsay felt like mowing down her gardens, but if he got caught that would have got him in more trouble than he would have wanted, for Mrs. Ho Sang and her husband had some very powerful friends in the government and business.

So he started after Bradford. He knew if he could catch Bradford doing something, he would have his revenge. But breaking things wasn't against the law.

He soon found out, though, that me and Bradford were smoking herb, and he knew if he caught us, he would get to

Mrs. Ho Sang. He had become a fanatic against herb smoking after his son, Kevin, who had been studying law at U.W.I., had a nervous breakdown. The boy was half-mad to begin with, and the herb just opened his eyes to the truth about him and his father. They found him two weeks after his breakdown near the clock in Cross Roads counting stones and saying, "One dollar, two dollar, three dollar," and every time he got to five dollars, he would throw the stones at the face of the clock and shout, "Death to the Pope, the Queen, Margaret Thatcher, Ronald Reagan, and Henry Kissinger!" He would then give a lecture on the conspiracy that these five had put together to destroy black people with AIDS.

His lectures always drew a crowd because they were filled with truths and half-truths about the five – sometimes we didn't know which was which – but they were always tinged with the trace of his own madness.

Well, we started to play it safe after one night when we were playing scrimmage soccer on the badminton court near our community centre. While we were playing under the lights, Corporal Ramsay crawled all the way from the community centre to the court, about fifty feet, on his belly to try and catch us. But his own excitement got to him and as he jumped up and said, "Aha, I catch you now!" Bradford swallowed the spliff, lighted butt and all.

Corporal Ramsay grabbed him by the neck and hollered, "Don't swallow it, don't swallow it," but Bradford made a giant swallow and everything went down.

The inside of Bradford's mouth was burned, but he wasn't arrested. Corporal Ramsay knew that if they got a good lawyer, and his mother would, he could get off easily on that. Corporal Ramsay wanted something big, something that would hurt.

From then on we started to smoke inside Bradford's room, right beside the toilet, so in case they tried to break down the door we could flush everything down the toilet. We would sit by the window, smoke a little herb, and flick the ash through the window. That way they couldn't even find a seed in the room if they tried. We weren't real ganja heads, but we hadn't passed enough "O" or "A" levels to go to the university, and our parents weren't rich enough to afford to send us to a university in the States. So we just stayed at home, smoked a little herb and flicked the ash through the window.

But it was our own caution that got us into trouble. Six months went by without Corporal Ramsay being able to pin anything on us. We would get random searches as we went to play soccer or cricket. Even when we were dressed up and going out, the man would search us. The man started to harass us, but we couldn't complain to our parents, for that would just lead to questions like, "So why is he searching you in the first place," and we didn't want that to happen. So we put up with it. We always smoked before we left the house. When he searched us, we just looked at him with our red eyes and laughed. Sometimes that would give us the giggles so much that he would leave us alone in the middle of a search. To us the whole thing seemed to be a big joke. One time Bradford, for no reason at all, started to laugh at Corporal Ramsay just because he saw him unpacking his groceries.

But one afternoon, Corporal Ramsay was driving by in his police car with another officer, who was taking him home, and he noticed something he couldn't believe. He parked the car, turned on the sirens and called the junior officer to join him. He walked over to Mrs. Ho Sang with his gun drawn and ordered her to turn around. The junior officer placed the handcuffs on her wrists.

With the sirens blaring, and Mrs. Ho Sang protesting, all the neighbours ran outside to see what was happening. We put out our spliffs, flushed them and came outside. When we got outside, we realised that Corporal Ramsay had got his revenge, and Mrs. Ho Sang still didn't know what was going on.

With all the commotion swirling around him, Corporal Ramsay pointed to a giant marijuana plant that had been growing in the croton hedge outside Bradford's window. We didn't even know it was there, for we were still buying from an old dread who lived in Standpipe. With all the fertilizers that Mrs. Ho Sang had used, the plant had grown at least five feet tall. The plant had big sturdy branches. Mrs. Ho Sang, who didn't know it was a marijuana plant, had been pruning it when Corporal Ramsay saw her. She liked it because it looked exotic and she liked the shape of its leaves. She even had some good-sized buds stuck in her hair as she stood by the police car with the blue and red lights shining in her face.

Corporal Ramsay stepped forward and looked her in the eyes.

"Is this your house?"

"You know that!" said Mrs. Ho Sang contemptuously.

"Be careful," cautioned Corporal Ramsay. "You can only make matters worse if you don't give us the information we want. Is this your house?"

"Yes, it's my house."

"Is this your garden?"

"Yes, Corporal Ramsay."

Corporal Ramsay then strode confidently over to the bushes, uprooted the marijuana plant and held it in his fist.

"Confess now that this is your marijuana plant, growing in your garden or we will find out whose room this is, dig up all these gardens for evidence, and who find out who else might have been growing it."

Mrs. Ho Sang was shocked. She looked over all her gardens, and saw Bradford in the crowd. He had tears running down his face.

"Don't do it, Mama. It's mine. Is mine."

Mrs. Ho Sang looked at him, and bowed her head while Corporal Ramsay growled, "Confess. Confess. Confess or we dig up all of them!"

"Its mine," she muttered.

"Officer, take her away," said Corporal Ramsay.

The junior officer took her to the back seat of the car and Bradford ran after his mother, "It's mine, Mama. It's mine. Corporal Ramsay, arrest me. Arrest me!"

"She's already confessed. Give it up," he said tersely.

The junior officer drove away in the car, and as the neighbours left and the sirens faded, Corporal Ramsay just stood there pleased with himself. Bradford just cried and cried and plotted his revenge.

Bradford plotted for a whole year while his mother retired to her gardens. That was her only pleasure now. But Bradford never got a chance to exact his own revenge. Corporal Ramsay was caught with some prostitutes from Knutsford Boulevard in New Kingston and his picture was printed in the *Star* and *Inquirer*. Because of the scandal and the way he handled Mrs. Ho Sang, he was fired from the force. The last time anyone saw him, he was a security guard at an ice cream factory. Even then, Bradford was still going after him until he had a dream and Haile Selassie appeared in the dream and told him, "Vengeance is mine". From then on, Bradford Ho Sang became a Rastaman, Chinese dreadlocks and all. As for me, I never smoke herb in front of an open window any more.

ALL GOD'S CHILDREN

Marlene Thomas sat by the window of the kitchen and sliced through the line of fat between the chicken's leg and thigh. Outside the fence, she noticed garbage cans strewn across the back yard. It was the third time this week the dogs had spilled the garbage and it was only Wednesday. If she had a gun, she would have tracked them down, shot them and left them rotting in the streets so the John Crows could eat their eyeballs. She had enough of cleaning up after them.

She had even soaked the cans in ammonia so the smell would drive the dogs away. But the brown mongrels weren't afraid of anything. They rammed their wrinkled snouts against the side of the can until they toppled it. Not that there was a lot of food inside the cans, just bone and gristle. But they had something to chew on.

Pulling a chair from under the dining room table, she rested her legs, and listened to the early morning meditations of Pastor Phillips, a radio Baptist preacher. She liked listening to him because he always had advice for young girls in her position, and he played her favourite gospel songs, "Jesus Is My Friend," and "We're Gonna Have A Grand Time Over In Zion." Besides, the music would calm her, for she didn't want to get angry, it would affect her baby. But she couldn't help it. When she looked down at her hands, the chicken was a bloody mess.

"Is what going on in here with all this chopping?" asked Lorna, her mother.

"I finish cutting up the chicken," said Marlene.

"More look like you murder it to me," said Lorna. "You don't think the bird dead enough already."

"I sorry. The dog turn over the garbage can again and I going have to clean it up."

"Is that bothering you? I wish my life was that simple. If it will help, I will clean it up for you. But, Child, you must control you temper, you know."

She hated to be scolded by her mother, and she waited for her to bring up the time when she lost her temper with a girl in school who had teased her and called her, 'Hermitage Gal'. The girl pulled the back of her uniform, and exposed her breasts to all the boys in the schoolyard. They told her later that she punched the girl in the eye and kicked her into unconsciousness. It was like an icy feeling came over her, and it wasn't the first time it had happened. This time the principal had no choice but to expel her.

She tried to change the subject, "Is okay, Mama. I will pick it up. Don't worry yourself. You already late for work, and you boss going faas with you if you late again."

It worked. Lorna was a garment cutter at a factory in the free-trade zone or, as she called it, "the slave-trade zone". Her boss, Mr. Robinson, told her if she came late one more time, he was going to fire her. Mr. Robinson was always threatening her, telling her how many other women outside the fence were dying to get her job. Not that she had a great job, but it paid the rent for her little cottage. She left at six every morning, and came home at ten at night. And that was if she made all the right mini bus connections.

Mr. Robinson had cornered her for sex several times, not because he liked her – there wasn't any love or desire on his part – but he wanted to show her that he was the boss. He wanted her because she was a woman who worked under him, and he had the power. He held the handle and she held the blade as her mother used to say. But Lorna would rather have died before she would allow any man, and especially an man like him, to huff and puff over her so she could keep her job.

"You don't worry about me," said Lorna. "Worry about what you going do about that baby you carrying."

Marlene turned around. She had a startled look on her face. "The bay... What baby?"

"Don't try, Girl. You think I don't know my own daughter. You think you can hide anything from your mother?"

Marlene was expecting the kind of lecture that her friend, Angela, had gotten before her mother threw her out of the house. She looked down at the apron tied around her waist.

"Marlene," said Lorna as she squeezed her daughter's arm, "I went to see Miss Prince, and she say she will do it for me. She will take care of the baby."

Marlene pulled her arm out of her mother's grip.

"What? What, Mama? You want me to go that obeah woman and kill my baby?"

"Don't say that! Don't make it sound like that," said Lorna. "So how I should make it sound, Mama?"

"I thinking about you, Marlene. You is my concern." Lorna gazed at her daughter's face. Marlene had the same intensity in her brow as her father. When Lorna told him she was going to have his baby, he disappeared and no one ever saw him in Bethel Town again. Lorna was left to take care of Marlene by herself, and she moved to Kingston to work as a maid. Lorna had vowed that she would never let Marlene slip up like her. Not like her. Not in this life. For what was the use of being her mother if her daughter was going to make the same mistake?

"You think I want to kill your baby?" she asked. " Is my baby too. You is my daughter and that child is a piece of me too. But that child is worries."

Marlene picked up the pieces of chicken and stuffed them in the pot with the sliced onion, garlic and vinegar that she had prepared earlier that morning. She would let the chicken soak in the fridge until she came home that evening.

"And I was here thinking you was going throw me out of the house," said Marlene.

"As long as you is my daughter, you will have somewhere to live. I not going see you living in the streets like you don't have nobody to take care of you. But this baby is a different thing."

Lorna picked up her sweater from the back of the chair where Marlene had been sitting. She had left it there the previous night before she collapsed in her bed.

"So where you was thinking of going in case I did chase you out. You think Dr. Hamilton, mind you, Dr. Anthony Hamilton, was going put you under the same roof with him son?"

"You know who the baby father is?" asked Marlene.

"Dr. Hamilton and me have a long talk last Saturday," said Lorna.

"Without me knowing? You was discussing me behind my back without me knowing?"

"You still a child, and there is some things that only big people can decide."

"Is still my life."

"I know. I know, Child. But I was trying to help you."

Lorna buttoned the front of her sweater and pulled up her collar. There was a slight chill in the October breeze that morning and it could get real cold on the waterfront. Marlene covered the pot with a rag and put it on the bottom shelf of the fridge.

"So what you and him decide?" she asked.

"Him give me five hundred dollars and tell me do what was best. So I asked him what should do with five hundred dollars? Then him start with his business about being a ministerial servant in the Jehovah's Witness, and that they don't believe in abortion. And a whole heap of horse dead and cow fat."

"And me and Gary don't have no say in what happen?" asked Marlene.

"Is not that, Marlene. Is not that. You have to face facts. You think a rich brown man like that who feel him belong to the right class and the right religion going have him only son marry a girl like you?"

"And what wrong with me?"

"Nothing at all, my child. Nothing at all. The only thing wrong with you is what wrong with this whole damned country. We poor and black and them rich and brown. You forget so soon that I used to work for them."

"Gary isn't like that," Marlene protested.

"But him father is. And him father not going allow it."

Marlene turned her back and started washing her hands in the sink. Chicken fat had gotten under her nails, and she lathered her hands carefully so they wouldn't smell. She wiped her hands in the apron and pulled it from around her waist.

"But Gary promised me."

"Never mind what him promise you. You have to be real. What happen if him father throw him out of the house. What you going do?"

"We already think about that. We would go down to the country and live with him grandfather. Him have a farm and Gary would become a farmer."

Lorna could not contain her laughter.

"Girl, listen to me and listen to me good. Go up to Miss Prince. That boy living in a fantasy world that you can't afford to live in."

"But he said..."

"Don't mind what he said. Listen to me. What that boy know about farming? Him ever work a day in him life? Farmer life is the toughest life you can live. Why you think Kingston have so much people? Why you think I move up here? If country life was so easy, you think all them people wouldn't be down in the country earning them bread? Girl, I beg you, go see Miss Prince."

Lorna walked over to Marlene, kissed her and tried to wipe away her tears.

She knew she wasn't telling her daughter the right thing,

just the best thing. She checked her purse for change and started through the door.

"Mama, I will have dinner ready for you when you come home," said Marlene.

"All right, Marlene. But you do what I tell you," said Lorna.

Lorna's footsteps were heavy, heavier than usual, and slower. But she was still strong enough for the walk up to the crossroads of August Town and University Road. Marlene watched her as she walked up the hill, then turned and left the apron on the back of the chair. She went inside her room to check her hair and the dress she was going to wear to see Gary. She took the dress off the hanger behind the door where she had hung a picture of Jesus with the Sacred Heart.

She spread the dress on the bed, carefully moving the pillow so she wouldn't crush the skirt. It was a navy blue dress with a starched white collar. She had borrowed her mother's white belt without her knowing, and she had bought a pair of white stockings to go with her new black, patent-leather shoes. Marlene had spent the night getting everything ready. She had borrowed the neighbour's steam iron, and ironed each pleat on the dress, and had sprinkled water around the waist of the dress so it wouldn't shine.

Marlene went around to the back of the house and took a shower. She powdered herself and put on her underwear. Her belly was still barely showing.

She'd been worried when she missed her period, for she was always regular. She didn't know what was happening. After the third month and the nausea, she went with Angela to the doctor. He did some tests and told her she was pregnant.

"But how..." Then she'd stopped herself when she saw the look on the doctor's face.

Marlene was so proud to have Gary's baby. He had chosen her when he could have had any girl he wanted. He was the headboy at Jamaica College and he played on the football team. And here she was, a girl who didn't finish high school.

Sometimes she thought she was going crazy when she thought about the baby. *Our baby.*

She dressed herself quickly, slipped on her stockings and shoes, and linspected herself in the mirror. She looked as if she was going to church.

She closed the door and started up the hill. As she passed the rum shops and off-course betting shops and the gatherings of men outside them – even though the shops weren't yet open, she saw Miss Prince outside the gate with her granddaughter. *Probably looking to work more obeah*, she thought.

Miss Prince waved to her, but she pretended she didn't see her and continued on the marl road up the hill. When she got to the crossroads, a minibus had pulled up and she got inside. It wasn't until she was halfway down Mona Road, she remembered the garbage. *Put out the garbage when you get home*, she reminded herself.

"One stop, driver," she shouted and she got off at Arailia Drive. From there it would be a short walk over to Palmoral Avenue where Gary lived.

She walked up to Dr. Hamilton's residence, which was on the corner, and halted under the shade of a pine tree where a mockingbird had built its nest that summer.

As she waited, she looked up at the former maid's quarters. It had been transformed into a small cottage that Dr. Hamilton rented to medical students at the University. A retired history teacher, he had redesigned his home so it no longer resembled the other square, boxy flats so common in Mona Heights.

Since his retirement, he spent his days working for his church, while his wife had planted, without much success, rows of daises and rose bushes down the sides of the walkway leading from the main house to the cottage.

Marlene knocked on the gate. The dogs barked from behind the house, and she realised that the Dobermans – Pluto and Rusty – had been chained, otherwise they would have been at the gate, teeth bared, froth dripping from their mouths.

She opened the gate and walked up to the house where she knocked on the second gate to the verandah and car port. She waited another five minutes before Doris, the maid who had taken her place, came out.

"Oh is you? Nobody not here."

"But Gary told me he was going to talk with me today."

"Well, Mr. Gary not here. Nobody not here. So go home. And show some respect when you talking about these people." Doris tried to close the door, but Gary's hand prevented her.

"Marlene, is that you," said Gary.

"But Mr. Gary, your father say..."

"Never mind what my father says. I'll take care of this." He opened the padlocks on the gate and let Marlene into the verandah where he offered her a seat on an adirondack chair. He sat down beside her. They sat in silence for ten minutes before Gary pulled his chair at a right angle to Marlene to glimpse her face. He covered his face with his palms and gazed through the grilled metal.

Eventually he spoke. "They're thinking of disfellowshipping me from the congregation."

"What that mean?" she asked.

"They will announce my name to the congregation and tell them that I was guilty of conduct unbecoming a Christian. I will have to sit at the back of the Kingdom Hall and no one can speak with me. I would be one of the world."

"And what about me? I was studying the Bible with you."

"You weren't a baptized member, so you don't get punished."

Marlene looked out at the pine tree and the nest which had been battered by the summer rain.

"And how long this go on?" she asked.

"Until I prove that I have changed my ways and repented my sins."

"But how long?" she asked again.

"It could take forever. I know a brother who wouldn't stop

drinking, no matter how many times they disfellowshipped him. They prayed and fasted with him, but he wouldn't stop. He kept on drinking until they threw him out for the last time, and he never came back to our congregation."

"Is he still a Christian?"

"No, he doesn't come to our congregation any more. He refused to sit in the back and be shunned."

"Why?"

"Because, like I told you, if you are disfellowshipped, no one is allowed to speak with you."

"Would you speak with me?" she said playfully.

Gary got up from the chair and looked down at the rose bushes whose dull green leaves lined the walkway. Their stems, thick with thorns, pushed out from the hard ground. He turned his back and lowered his head.

"So are you really pregnant?" he asked.

"Yes," she said. "Our baby's fine. What you want? A boy or a girl?"

"How can you ask me that? Haven't you heard what I said?"

"Yes, no one from your church will talk to you. So, we have each other, and we can go to another church," she said.

"You mean another congregation? " asked Gary. "It would be the same. I would have to transfer my records there."

"No, I mean we would go to another church," said Marlene.

"There is no other church. We are the true church. I can't go anywhere else. Didn't I teach you that when we were studying the Bible together?"

"You teach me a whole heap more than that," she teased and reached for his hand.

His hand went limp and he placed her hand on the arm of the chair. He wanted to squeeze her hand tightly, but decided he had to be strong as his father had told him.

"What we did was wrong. Wrong. Wrong. I gave in to temptation and now I have to pay the price for my sins. Don't you see?"

"If you say so. But you said everything was going to be all right. You said we would go down to the country if things went bad up here."

"I never figured on this. My grandfather is an elder in the congregation down there. I have nowhere to go."

"So it was all lies," said Marlene. "All you were doing was telling me lies."

"No, it wasn't lies. I never told you any lies!"

"So what was it, Gary? What was it?"

Gary held onto the side of the grilled gate. The sun had flaked the corners where the wrought iron met the concrete.

"How could you have gotten me in this position?" he said.

"Me? What position I get you in, Gary? What position? You said you wanted to make love. We make love. You teach me God is love."

"But not that kind of love."

"Love is love, Gary."

"That's not what my congregation thinks."

"Then, them wrong."

Turning slowly to face her, amazed and angry that she could have said something like that, he said, "My father was right. You wouldn't understand our way."

"Before, you used to tell me it was mine and your way. Now you telling me is you and your father way, after the two of them go behind our back and discuss us."

"They were thinking about our best interests."

"Best interest to dash away my baby?"

"My father would never suggest anything like that. Maybe your mother would, but he would never think about anything like that."

"So why did he give her five hundred dollars. What five hundred dollars can do. What him did expect?"

"He was trying to protect me. He said maybe the baby wasn't mine."

Marlene felt her mouth go dry. Her nipples felt cold. She got up from the chair. The pleats on her dress were ruined.

"The baby wasn't yours? The baby wasn't yours? So whose could it be? The Holy Ghost? We were supposed to be studying the Bible together when you started to feel around and touch me. I didn't know what to do."

"I thought a girl like you knew what to do?"

"A girl like me? What? You mean because I come from Hermitage, I supposed to know everything about sex? I never know a thing. Not a thing. I was a virgin. A virgin."

"So was I," he said. "So was I." He looked away. He picked a piece of crusted paint off the gate.

"So it wasn't true, then," said Marlene. "You never love me. You never love me at all. You only wanted to use me."

"No, I would never do that. It wasn't like that at all."

"Well, say is our baby."

The door swung open and Dr. Hamilton motioned to his son.

"I've heard enough. You, young lady, I want you to leave the premises at once. You've caused enough problems here."

"What trouble, Sir?"

"You don't call seducing my son, causing him to face disciplinary charges in front of the other elders and the embarrassment it has caused us trouble? Look at the pain you've caused? No, no, no. I'm asking you to leave. Leave now and don't come back."

"And if I come back?"

"Look, I've given your mother the money for whatever involvement my son had with you. It's more than you're worth, but he's made his mistake. Now I'm asking you to leave before I call the police to take you away."

"You would do that, Sir? You would call police on me and your grandchild?"

"That is not my grandchild. Go back to Hermitage to your real baby-father. Let him take care of your pickney. Breed as much as you want. But don't come back to my house or I will set the dogs on you."

"The dogs?" said Marlene and looked around. She put her skirt between her legs. "You would do that, Sir? Call the dogs on your own grandchild? You would let him do that to your son, Gary? To your own son or daughter?"

"You don't have to answer that, Son," said Dr. Hamilton. "Get inside now."

"But..."

"Now," said Dr. Hamilton as he pushed Gary inside the house and closed the door behind them.

"Tell him, tell him," screamed Marlene. "Tell him is your baby. Your baby, Gary."

The door clicked, and Dr. Hamilton closed the dead bolt. He yelled at Gary, "And it wasn't the fact that she was the maid why I'm so angry, but she so damned black." Goose bumps nettled Marlene's flesh. She couldn't feel anything.

"I going to get the dogs," said Dr. Hamilton, and she could hear his steps at the back of the house. He was opening the door in the kitchen.

Marlene heard the gate to the kitchen open. Soon the dogs would be out. She rushed toward the gate. She had just closed it behind her when Pluto mounted the fence. Rusty followed and began barking at her. She turned and faced them. Sensing her lack of fear, they jumped off the fence, but continued barking at her.

Her arms were numb and her legs tingled. "Say is your baby," she mumbled as she turned away from the house. "Say is your baby. *Our baby.*"

She walked stiffly down Palmoral Avenue to Mona Road, caught a minibus and headed home. The ice settled in her belly. The houses breezed past the windows of the minibus. She looked up at the hills and the caverns gouged out by bulldozers until she recognised the familiar stench of Hermitage. She got out at the crossroads, marched past the men who were already drunk inside the rum shops and went straight to Miss Prince's house. The stones on the marl road crackled under her soles. The house had just been swept and the dust mounted the handle of a pitcher and an enamel basin on a table in the living room where the old woman was sitting. Miss Prince looked at her as if she had been expecting her.

"Whatever you going do, do it now, and do it quick," said Marlene.

"Yes, me child," said Miss Prince. "I will do it for you," and held her in her arms as she had done with Marlene's mother before her, and sent her granddaughter to prepare the bitter herb.

MY BROTHER'S KEEPER

When Papa dead, I cry till I almost vomit. I never know I would miss him that much because I used to never see him plenty, even when him was alive. I used to see him during Christmas when him would come back from Belle Glade in Florida. I can't even remember him face. I remember that him was a tall, bowlegged man who used to make some chaka-chaka sound when him eat. So when Ma tell me that Papa dead in a car accident in Miami with some woman, and that me have a little brother name David, I couldn't believe it. But when Ma tell me that the boy was going live with me and share my bed. I know I was going hate the boy even before I meet him.

I don't like hating people, but when him step in through the door with him new bag, new shoes, new shirt, and new pants, and me sit down there in the living room, barefoot and tear-up, tear-up, I hate him even more. Worse, him was wearing the watch that Papa did promise to give me the last time him leave at Christmas.

Papa did say as soon as him get back to America, him would send the watch to me in the mail. Him say him would wrap it up tight tight so them thiefing people at the post office wouldn't take it out and keep it for themself.

Now the watch wasn't a fancy watch with gold or anything like that. It was just a regular Timex, but it had a calculator and timer and a whole heap a thing me would never use. But nobody else on the block, not even Richard Chin Sang, who

62

used to get me in trouble with Ma, and who used to think that him was better than everybody else, including me, had one. I ask the boy for the watch, and explain to him that Papa did promise the watch to me, and that him should just hand it over to me there and then. You know what that little idiot have the nerve to say? **No.** I did feel like to just box him over him head, and take it way, but I never want to get into any more trouble with Ma, so I just let it be. It was then I decide, fly high, fly low, I was going to get that watch. Papa did say it did belong to me. It was mine.

So the boy start to unpack and everybody start to make a fuss over him like him was Marcus Garvey son. I couldn't believe the fuss that them was making over that little red 'kin boy. It was like Ma never realise that the only way that him could be my brother is that Papa was sleeping with another woman, probably the woman who him dead with. And from the look of that boy, it was probably a white woman. I guess it never sink in, for if anybody did do that to me, orphan or no orphan, him would be out in the street.

But that is Ma problem and where me an she different. She always take up these hardluck stories and trying to save people and change the world. That is why her brother, Uncle George, living with us. Him used to own a bar down in Papine till him drink off all the profit. Now, everyday him getting drunk. So when the boy take out a present for him and it was a bottle of Johnny Walker from the States that him aunt, who couldn't take care of him any more, send with him, eye water start to run down the man face and him say, "This is a good boy, Doreen. A good boy. David, I want you to stay out of trouble and don't follow that little hooligan over there. I love you boy. I love you."

Uncle George would love anybody who give him a drink. That old rumhead fool will say anything for a Appleton and when thing get bad, bay rum. But the boy take him serious and start to hug the old rum head. And Uncle George hugging him

63

back and bawling. Everybody forget that is me always have to fetch Uncle George, sometime in the worse bar in Kingston, clean him up, and take him home.

Then the boy start to take out all the trophy him win in school in Miami. Basketball trophy, baseball trophy, football trophy, and Uncle George, who start the bottle already, rubbing the boy head and saying, "Doreen, this boy is a athlete!" And Ma put all the trophy on the dresser. My dresser. Then Ma begin to cry and say how strong him was and that Papa was strong too. She hug the boy and leave me in the room with the trophy. I feel like break every single trophy on the dresser, but I know if I did ever do that it wouldn't be Ma who would beat me, it would be Uncle George and him beat hard. Since the last time him beat me, I never want him to beat me again. And especially when him drunk, which is all of the time. Ma you can fool with a little scream, but with Uncle George you could bawl and scream as loud as you want, "*Lord, Lord, Lord God! Stop! I not going do it again. I not going do it again. I promise. I promise. I promise you. I promise you I won't do it again. I going dead now, I going dead. Lord, Lord, Lord God, Lord God!*" him wasn't going stop until him was done. And then dog eat you supper.

So I just look at the trophy them and pass aside. All them trophy. Me never get a trophy in my life for nothing. The one thing that me know me can do good is bird shooting, and you don't get trophy for bird shooting. Plus Ma make me stop because one time I kill a mockingbird. Now I was only trying to help because every morning, before she had to go to school, she would wake up and say how this mockingbird was waking her up at five o'clock in the morning and that she couldn't get a good night sleep. So I wake up early one morning and as the bird open him mouth, baps, him dead. So I walk into the kitchen big and broad with the dead bird, but Ma start to cry and give me this long speech how I was wicked to shoot a bird during mating season and that God was going to punish me and I was going to hell. She made me feel so bad. All I wanted to do was help her, but it never worked. But that is just how Ma is, you can never understand her.

Even my father could never understand her and that is why him leave the last time. I know she did really love him, but I know that they was married because of me. How I know is one time Papa and Ma get into a big fight and Papa lick Ma.

Well, she phone Uncle George and him come to the house with him gun. Them have a few words and Papa say something and then Uncle George say something.

Then Papa say him would never marry Ma if it wasn't for me. And then Uncle George slam the door and I think him pull the gun. That is how I find out that I was a bastard.

Anyway, *that* bastard was back here in my room, and Ma was running her hand through him hair and saying how straight it was and how him was so light skin. Uncle George was patting him on the shoulder and looking at him teeth.

Uncle George don't have a teeth in him head. Him lose all of them by fighting and the rest of them rotten out and him have to pull them. But this boy did have all him teeth, and some with gold fillings too. That impress Uncle George. Me, I lose two in a fight, and I never been to a dentist, though me is sixteen years old. I don't think I ever going to one.

Ma hug him again and say she was going to fix dinner and if him did like chicken. Him say yes and Ma just wrap him up in her bosom and give him that smile that you couldn't help but smile. But I never smile. I just show him where him could put the rest of him things. Uncle George say I was jealous, but what did that old rumhead know?

One thing I can say about the boy though, him was hard to fool. Him wasn't like me cousin, Owen, from the country who me did lock in the closet. I tell Owen it was a elevator and him believe me. As him step inside, I just lock the door and keep him in there for about a hour until Uncle George hear the knocking and run come inside the room. I let out Owen right away. When I see Uncle George, I tell him we was just playing, and I guess him never feel like beat me that day, and him believe me. But this one you couldn't fool. I try, but it never work. Him was smart. Him was dangerous.

So I leave him in the room and run down the street to meet my friend over by the park. As I jump over the fence, I hear these footstep behind me. I chase the boy back to the yard. I tell him that him couldn't come because him was wearing him new shoes. Him say the shoes wasn't new, them was six months old. Real American. I tell him that him couldn't come and play and wear the watch, for it could break. Him say it was shock proof. I tell him that him would have ask Ma first before him leave, and it was then him have the gall to call my mother, my own mother, "Ma," to my face. I tell him there and then that she was my mother. She wasn't him mother. Him did have a mother of him own, and that whoever she was and wherever she was, him should go find her. I tell him if him ever call her Ma in front of me again, I don't care what Uncle George would do to me, I was going to beat the shit out of him.

Him walk off and start to bawl, but I never care, for him wouldn't be trailing me all around the place, so that all my friend would laugh after me.

When I get back home that night though, it was bangarang. Ma start to give me a long speech about how I must think about my little brother feelings and after what I learned in Sabbath school about Cain and Abel. She go on for about a hour about the Sabbath school business. Sabbath school. I only used to go there to please her because she always talking about how she going to dead and how she want me to grow up to be a good man. Good man, good woman. Them things dead from the start. She is a good woman and look where it get her. A little elementary schoolteacher in Back O' Wall or whatever they call it now. Good woman. The only thing that worth is a whole heap a pain and a little boy following you around the place and asking questions about, "What's this?" and "Why do they call it that?" while all you friend laughing after you. Which is what

I have to put up with because Ma say so. What nearly kill me, though, is that she say him could call her Ma if he wanted to. She say it. I hear it from her own mouth. But I take one look at him and him never do it in front of me.

So the next day me and him was walking down the street and him start telling me story about how Papa take him to Disney World, how Papa this and how Papa that, and I never want to hear it. And then him tell me how Papa dead and how him cry and cry, and him glad that I was him brother. And that was why him want to keep the watch because it remind him of Papa. It was then I know how much I hate him, for nobody could love Papa like me.

When we get to the park, I tell him to keep him mouth shut. I never want my friend to find out that him was me brother. But as we step through the gate, Richard Chin Sang say, "Who that with you, Umpire?" Umpire is my nickname, but that is another whole long story. Before Richard could finish the question, the little idiot shout out, "I'm his brother."

Well, everybody start to laugh because him never look anything like anybody in my family and Richard say him must be a *jacket*. Richard did want to change my name from Umpire to 'Three Piece Suit and Thing'. 'And Thing' would be David.

But Richard wouldn't have him way. Me and him did fall out from the time him try to tell a lie on me and it backfire. Richard used to thief for nothing. One day me and him was in the staff room at school and him thief ten dollars from a teacher purse. Them find out that it was only me and him who was in the room that morning, so it must be one of us. Richard say him don't need the money for him bring at least thirty dollar to school every week. And him pull out the thirty dollar.

So everybody say it must be me. I nearly end up with a caning because everybody know I used to get into a whole heap of fight and they say I was a troublemaker. Now I couldn't get a caning, for if you get a caning they call your house. Then I have to go home to face Uncle George and get another whipping. So I take everybody to the other end of the school where I know Richard used to hide all the things him used to steal. When they open the locker, comb, toothbrush, chewing gum, even somebody slide rule fall out. He never need them, but him thief them. So they suspend him from school, and when him get home, him father beat him so hard him never come out for three week. It was from then me and him never get along. So the truth come out, but it never set me free. Even my friend Peter from up the road did try to call me, 'Three Piece Suit' because him did know I couldn't get into any more fight. But I tell him if he ever called me that, I would tell Laura Spenser father what them was doing at the Christmas fair behind the Ferris wheel. I had to threaten all of them like this, for I know everything about all of them, but they don't know a thing about me. I always make sure people owe me, not me owe them or them have anything on me. Just because I can't fight anymore, don't mean that anybody can take steps with me. I keep everything to myself, but this little idiot was going to mash up everything. I never like that.

But him did have some use. In time we teach him how to play cricket and football. Him call it soccer. Teaching him to play cricket was a joke. The boy lick four runs, drop the bat and start to run like him hear news. We just tell him to pick up the bat, and tell him that it wasn't baseball him was playing. We teach him how to hold the bat, to dip and score runs. It did take time, but him learn.

But the best thing was all them trophy that him did get from basketball. Him never play football good, so we put him in the goal. Papa, now that was a goalkeeper. From the ball land in him hand, that done. Him catch it. From that day on, Richard Chin Sang and him friend never score a goal on we. We beat them team ten games straight. That never happen before. Every Saturday them used to just win all the games and send we home with a bus ass. But when we start to win, them did want stop play with we, but them soon realise that if them did really want a good game of football, even though them never like we, them would have to play against we. Now, don't get me wrong, is not that I did start to like the boy, but we was winning, and that make a difference.

So when we start win all the game, everybody else start to like him. Sometime I wish them did call we 'Three Piece Suit and Thing'. But all of them forget. People have short memory, especially when them is your friend. Peter even wanted to call David, 'Little Umps' but I put and end to that too. I wasn't sharing my name with him.

But everything broke loose one evening after a football game. I had to go help Uncle George get home. Him was drunk again. And it was a bar way down in Hermitage. So I had to get him and clean him up. When I finally find him, it was about seven o' clock and by the time we get home it was eight-thirty. Just as I finish clean him up and put him in the bed, Peter little sister run inside the house and tell me that David in a fight with Richard. I just take me time, for I know David couldn't take on Richard and win. Him was finally going get the bus ass that him should get from the first day him step inside my house.

By the time I get to the park, Richard was holding the boy like a piece of stick and licking the boy in him face. Well, sooner or later the boy would have to learn, and I wasn't going to get into any fight for him. If I was going to get in a fight, it would be my fight. And whoever I fight would have to be worth the beating I would get when I go home. This boy wasn't worth it.

When Richard see me, him stop and pretend like nothing was going on. But when him see that I wasn't going help the boy, him lick the boy so hard I feel it down to me shoes. Is then I find out what the fighting was about. Richard hold him and say, "See, I tell you, him afraid of me. Him not going fight for you. Him don't even like you."

"I still say," David was shouting, "he can beat you up any day."

The little idiot. Him was fighting to defend me name. Some people never learn. You shouldn't say things, even if they true, if you can't back them up with your fist. Richard throw him down on the ground and kick him in him side. Now that wasn't right. Beating up somebody is one thing, but when you kick them on the ground is another. But it wasn't my fight.

Then Richard tear off the watch off David hand and was going crush the face with the heel of him shoes, and David bawl out, "I'll give you the watch, Paul. But don't let him break Papa's watch."

And as Richard foot come down, the boy dive underneath it and take the heel in him chest. Him really did love Papa.

Well, before Richard know what happen, I sucker punch that Chinee boy so hard, him was seeing Chop Suey. Him stagger for about two yard and then I lick him cross him face with my fist. Him get a good blow to my face and bloodup me nose. But I kick him in him seed and him fall down and then start to run to him yard, bawling like a dog and saying him was going call me house and tell them what I do to him.

Is then I know I dead. Uncle George was going beat me this time. I was dead. I couldn't hide my nose with the blood; it was all over my shirt. Even if I could bribe David not to tell – although I never know with what, I never have anything on him – Richard was going to tell him father. Then him father would call my mother and embarrass her with, "What kind of wild animal you have there in your house that you calling your son? If you see what he do to my son and bla, bla, bla, bla, bla." I might as well run away from home.

I pick him up off the ground and clean him up. I help him wash him face with the hose near the badminton court. It was the first time I see him face. Him look at me and say, "I hope Ma doesn't beat you too hard when we get home,"

I almost forgive him for calling her Ma that time.

"Here, take this," him say and try to give me the watch. I couldn't take it. The boy earn it. I push him hand away and tell him to keep it. As we was walking home though, I ask him if I could borrow the watch every now and then. Maybe I could borrow it for the Christmas fair, if I was still alive. Him say yes and as we turn the corner, I look on the verandah and I see Uncle George, drunk and holding onto one of the column with one hand and the belt in the other. I know I was dead.

I couldn't run away, I never have anywhere else to go. And if I run away, I would have to come back, and the beating would still be waiting on me. I would probably get it worse then. I couldn't do a thing. I could only hope that him was too drunk to stand up and that him would fall asleep or throw up before him finish. But what if him remember that him never finish tonight and start on me tomorrow morning?

David see the look on me face, and run straight up to the verandah. Him start to cry and say how if it wasn't for me how them was going to mash up Papa watch. And him tell some lie about what them was calling Ma, all kind of bad word me never know the boy know. Then him say that Richard and him friend was running joke about Uncle George, that him is a rum head and how me rescue him from Richard and three of him friend. Three of him friend! The boy was good. It did sound so real. Me was there and even me did start believe it. The boy put on one show. Uncle George drop the belt, hug me and say, "For the first time, you do good, boy. You do good." Ma kiss me, rub me head, then take him inside. And all the while him smiling and winking with me. I couldn't believe it. It end up that me owe him. The little idiot save me.

THIN LINE

The morning sun lurked behind the shaded front of Jah B's Restaurant as the bass from three triple-eighteen-inch speakers rattled the locks on the shutters of the adjacent pawn shop. Bits of shattered glass and broken beer bottles crackled under Bruce's shoes as he walked down the sidewalk of the Liberty City Mini Mall. The stores, some of which were still boarded up since Hurricane Andrew to prevent further looting, were grilled with ornate metalwork and braced for summer storms.

He stepped inside Jah B's to get some breakfast and to wait until the pawnshop opened. The smell of stewed beef, jerk chicken and curried goat mingled with the shadows inside the restaurant.

Bruce sat on a stool by the entrance away from the other two customers in the restaurant. It was only eight-thirty and the men had already finished at least a six-pack of beer between them. Norman and Eddy were truck drivers and early morning regulars at Jah B's. Eddy wore a woollen tam and a faded denim jacket, while Norman wore a light green shirt, dark green slacks and a visored cap which covered most of his face. Bruce leaned over the counter and ordered his food.

"A patty and a Coke, please."

The old Chinese woman wasn't listening. She was too busy counting the tips left by last night's customers. When she saw Bruce, she stuffed the money into her apron and mumbled something to her son, Peter, who was talking with the cook's daughter, Mabel. Peter ignored her and went with the girl into the storage room.

"Can I help you?"

"A patty and a Coke, please," Bruce repeated as he lifted his knapsack, laden with textbooks, and placed it on the counter beside the condiments. He took two dollars from the left side pocket of the knapsack and paid for the food. The old woman gave him his change which he left on the counter. He slipped the patty out of the brown paper bag and cleaned the top of the Coke can. Just as he was about to bite into the patty, Eddy, shouted, "Mind what you eating inside here. You can never tell what you will get inside places like this. Just because is America don't mean that these Chinese people, when they low on cash, won't slip in some dog meat or road-kill every now and then. They did it in Jamaica, and they will do it here."

Bruce did not respond. He ignored the man and bit into the patty. Flakes fell over the front of his shirt. He brushed them off and continued eating.

"Wait," said Norman, "the boy not even listening to you."

"What did you expect, Norman, you don't hear how the boy order him food."

"*A patty and a Coke please* like him is a real American. I tell you, these young boys they come to America, and them forget everything. Forget the struggle, forget the suffering, forget them roots. Them forget everything and turn into American college boys who don't know shit."

"I hear you, Eddy, I hear you," said Norman. "I bet you him even *se habla español*, a real brown man like him."

Bruce sipped the Coke and took another bite of the patty.

"Hey," Eddy raised his voice a bit higher, "we talking to you. See what I mean, Norman, they even stop respecting their elders. You see that's another thing about this country: nobody respect their elders. Is that what you want, college boy, to stop respecting your elders."

Norman laughed and rubbed his elbow against Eddy's side.

Bruce said nothing. He drew his knapsack closer to his side and held the straps in his fist.

"You think you too good to talk with us, college boy. Too educated to talk with us," Norman taunted.

Eddy banged his fist on the counter and got off his stool. The old woman scurried through the side door and knocked on the door to the storage room.

"Peter, come here quick," she pleaded as she scurried through the side door leading to the kitchen. .

Peter called from the back room, "An you, Eddy and Norman, if is trouble you looking for, well, go look for trouble somewhere else. The two of you disturbing my customers."

Eddy pulled the woollen tam off his head and his locks fell to his shoulders. He twirled the ends of his hair with his fingers.

Peter walked out of the stockroom, straightening his collar and zipping up the front of his pants. He stood beside Bruce and banged his fist against the adding machine.

"Hey, Peter," said Norman, "We was just having a little fun with the boy here. We wasn't looking to disturb anybody, especially that pretty young thing you been eyeing ever since she put her foot through the door. You better make sure that the old lady don't find out though, because she might just tell your wife. Remember what happen the last time with the court business and all of that money the both of you lose before you decide to forget the divorce? She might just cut it off this time, you know, like that American girl do to her husband. Like one of these nights, you lying down in bed all peaceful and calm, and baps, it gone, never to come back again."

The old woman, who had come out to the counter again, shook her head disapprovingly.

"Eddy, me is a big man. Me can take care of meself. But this here is a youth, him barely out of the egg and you want to fast with him. Leave him alone."

"But, Peter, me and Norman was just wondering how

college boy would handle himself with that girl over there. Like if them would just hold hand and look at the stars. You know, like college boy, you ever see pussy before? I bet all you can do is read about pussy. I bet if one of these days, pussy was to look you in the face and say, *Here, take it,* you would probably run, eh, college boy. Run like you hear news. Yeah, you'd probably run, for what does a college boy know about pussy, about life?"

The two men finished their beers and left a tip on the counter. They patted Peter on the shoulder and snickered as they walked past Bruce and left the store.

"Sorry about that. But those guys have been working all night delivering goods. They come in here for a few beers, blow off a little steam and go home to their wives. They really didn't mean any harm," said Peter apologetically.

"Thanks, Mr. Chin. Thanks a lot. I was really getting worried."

"Its okay, College Boy. Take it easy. Hey, this place too dead. I going put on some music, and make everybody feel better."

He slipped a cassette into the tape deck behind him. There was a low droning noise before the music began: *Guiltiness rest on their conscience, oh yeah. These are the big fish who always try to eat down the small fish.*

Bruce took another sip of Coke and his eye caught an advertisement for the fourth annual Goombay festival in Coconut Grove. He picked up the flyer, and crumpled the paper into a ball. It was so simple to crush the paper, no matter the importance, the paper could be discarded.

And they would do anything to materialize their every wish. Oh, oh, yeah.

The song crackled through the speakers. The festival would have been three days of reggae, soca, calypso or any other island music the tide brought in. It would have been three days of escaping Miami without having to pay the air fare. It would have been three days with his mother and sister, if the rain hadn't fallen and ruined everything.

Miami was so strange! Everything came so quickly and easily without warning, even the rain. The storms gusted in from the ocean, and everything was drenched. It wasn't like Jamaica where the clouds gathered slowly, and got blacker and heavier until it seemed as if they were going to fall out of the sky. And the thunder. It sounded like a huge oil drum rolled across a river bed. Then there was the overhead flight of swallows before the sooncome of showers. But even then, there was enough time to get to shelter, for the hills usually held back the rain for some time, even after the first raindrop fell on the back of your neck, before the first breeze tore through the almond trees.

Things were different in Miami. After the first drop, everything was soaked to the marrow. It had happened to him so many times when he had just arrived. He would start walking from Johnson Street over to the Hollywood Fashion Center, and he would always end up being caught in mid-summer rain. That was seven years ago when his family had just moved here. Before that his father, who had worked so hard, left his job in the civil service and became a manager in a shoe store. It was then things started to change, almost without warning. It began slowly at first: his father started to drink harder and swore louder. Poor Dad.

Last summer, he had followed the smell of his father's whisky-soaked shirt to his sister's room and saw his father asleep with his hands inside her blouse. She was awake and there were tears running down the sides of her face. She made no sound when she saw Bruce, for she was afraid her father would awaken and he would start again. And she feared for Bruce. When he told his mother about it, she said that his father was only being affectionate, and kissed him on the forehead, careful to avoid hurting her bruised cheekbones.

Yet the festival would at least have given them a little peace. His father was going down to Jamaica for a funeral and Bruce had saved four hundred dollars from his work-study programme. He kept three hundred dollars for spending money and gave his mother one hundred dollars to buy herself some new outfits. His father never bought anything for her now. He only complained that he was forced to leave Jamaica because he couldn't stand the politics and violence, only to come to this place where he had to start all over again, to beg and scrape for every penny he earned. He said he was spending money on children that, for all he cared, probably weren't his. Bruce knew better.

The festival would have meant so much. It would have meant so much if he hadn't come home and found his mother lying unconscious in the dining room, her dress ripped at the seams. It would have meant so much if he hadn't seen his sister crying in the in the corner, unable to utter a syllable.

Woe to downpressors, they eat a bread of sad tomorrow. Oh, oh yeah...

Bruce gulped a mouthful of Coke and looked up at the clock. It was nine o'clock. Peter had opened the pawnshop.

Bruce took the last bite of the patty and swallowed the bits of hard gristle that were rubbing against the flat of his tongue. He reached inside the knapsack, took out three hundred dollars from the right side pocket, and walked over to the pawnshop.

The bell over the door rang, and Peter, looking a bit surprised, buzzed the lock for the second door and let him in. Bruce took out his driver's license and social security card.

"I called you yesterday about the revolver."

"That was you, College Boy?"

"Yes."

"You sounded different. But why you want a gun, College Boy?"

"Mr. Chin, you know better than to ask a question like that! This is Miami. Anything can happen. A storm or another riot could happen here tomorrow. You just have to be prepared."

"I know, College Boy, I know. I have my own protection too."

Bruce smiled while Peter checked his identification and asked him the mandatory questions.

Peter handed Bruce the gun. and said, "Congratulations!"

Bruce put the gun in his knapsack. He could feel the grooves of the barrel against his forefinger.

"Walk good, College Boy."

Bruce didn't hear him. He opened the doors of the pawn-shop, hesitated, looked up at the sky and then ran between the parked cars outside the restaurant. Before he reached the parking lot, raindrops were ricocheting off the cars.

"What do you call a faggot in a wheelchair with AIDS?" said Carlos.

"Don't know," said Basil.

"Rolaids," laughed Carlos. "Get it, ROLL-AIDS."

"Yeah, yeah, I got it," said Basil and handed him an aluminium panel. Carlos screwed a bolt into the top of the panel and then secured the sides with a thin metal strip.

"So you think it's gonna hit us?" asked Carlos.

"You never know with these things," said Basil. "It's like they have a mind of their own."

"Coño," said Carlos as he dismounted the ladder and packed his tools. Basil helped him to carry the ladder to campus security and they walked over to the lake where they always ate lunch.

They sat on the concrete benches overlooking a fountain that on sunny days sprayed a plume of water into the air, higher than the crown of the Royal palms that lined the mossy banks of the lake.

"I wonder what happened to the ducks," said Carlos as he unwrapped a Cuban sandwich he had bought at Aurora's Restaurant.

"They've found somewhere safe," said Basil. "When I used to live in the country, that's how we used to tell if a storm was coming. All the birds roost in the top of the house and the highest trees they could find. It's like they know there's going to be a flood, and they're getting as far away as possible."

"That's weird," said Carlos. "Birds and nature. It's like they know shit we don't."

A security guard on an electric cart stopped and honked his horn. Ramon and Humberto, their co-workers, jumped off the back of the cart. The security guard drove off and honked his horn again, but they were too tired to wave. They had been working for ten hours securing the campus against the hurricane which was approaching Miami.

Ramon opened a can of Coke and Humberto sat on the bench beside Basil and waited for him to open his lunch box.

"Who did this?" asked Basil, and he dropped his lunch box. There was a dead rat inside.

The men laughed and slapped their thighs. Ramon laughed so hard, Coke spewed out his nose, and he started to choke.

"I hope you drown," said Basil. "This isn't funny. This isn't funny at all."

"Oh, yes it is," said Carlos. "You should have seen your face! Like you'd seen a ghost or something. You were a riot."

Humberto nodded in agreement. He rarely said anything. He was the new guy in the group and Basil wondered if he spoke any English. The only words he had heard him speak were, "*Yes, No, lunch,* and *quitting time,*" and he spoke those with such a thick Cuban accent it still sounded like Spanish.

"Dead rats aren't funny," said Basil. "Which one of you guys did this?"

They all pointed at each other and laughed again. He should have known better. They were going to stick together. No matter how trivial, those guys always stuck together. He'd never get anything out of them.

"So where's my lunch?" he asked Carlos.

"I got it, Man," said Carlos and pulled a package wrapped in tin foil from the bottom of his lunch box.

"Hey, hold it for me. My beeper's going off," said Basil. He looked at the number and signaled that he'd received the call. "I'll get it from you when I come back. My wife's calling me."

"What does she want? " asked Carlos.

"Who the hell knows," said Basil and looked down at his beeper.

He really didn't need a beeper, but all the other guys had one so he decided to get one. When he'd bought it, his wife, Sheila, had asked him why he'd bought it. He told her he bought it so she could contact him at any time. She believed him and now he regretted that he'd bought it.

The guys on the bench were making all sorts of faces and gesturing with their hands. He deserved that. He'd played many tricks on them, hiding their tools, sending them fake memos and bogus beeper calls. He had earned the reputation of being a practical joker. But Sheila didn't like it. She said he was hiding his frustration at being passed over for promotion so many times. He'd been working for the college for six years and he had been passed over three times. Carlos, who had been hired a year after him, was now his supervisor, and Carlos didn't know anything. Carlos was always asking him how to do the simplest jobs. That was how he discovered Basil was afraid of rats. Basil was helping Carlos repair some duct work in the crawl space above the third floor of the administration building and a rat fell from inside the drywall and landed on him. He scurried out of the crawl space and wouldn't go back up there, no matter how much overtime Carlos offered him. He had always been afraid of rats and no one could persuade him to go near those things.

But now if he didn't watch it, Humberto would soon have Carlos's job. Carlos was going to a new job downtown, and he would be stuck in the same position for the rest of his life.

"Hurry! We got rat's ass sandwich for you," said Carlos. He held the dead rat by the tail and threw it near the lake. The rat plopped down into the marshy banks.

Carlos took another sip of his drink and watched Basil dial, speak for a while, then hang up the phone.

"Where's my lunch?" he said as he walked towards them.

"Take it easy, man," said Carlos. "I got it right here. You know everyone's afraid of rats, but not like you. You're paranoid!"

Carlos handed him a bag with Jamaican patties wrapped in foil.

"What's wrong man? Your old lady again? She gonna leave you?"

"I'd be so lucky," said Basil. "She's Catholic, she'll never leave me."

"So what's wrong?"

"Julian," said Basil.

Carlos didn't want to say anything because of his joke about gays.

"What's wrong?" asked Ramon.

"He doesn't have anywhere to stay. They're evacuating the beach, so my wife invited him to stay with us until the hurricane blows over."

"But I thought you threw him out and told him never to come back?"

"I did, but my wife changed my mind for me," said Basil.

"That's what mothers are for," said Carlos, "to love you no matter what."

"Well, I'm not a mother," said Basil.

"No, you're a *real* mother," said Carlos.

Basil smiled nervously. They all knew why he'd thrown Julian out of his house. They'd all seen the pictures in *The New Times* of his son in drag. Julian was mugging for the camera and pretending to have fun with his little faggot friends.

"So what are you going to do?" said Carlos.

"I don't know. He's brought one of his friends," said Basil with a lisp.

"Man, I don't know what I would do if my son told me he was gay," said Carlos. "I would kill him. Kill him right there."

"Don't judge these gays. I once had a homosexual experience," said Humberto. They all stared at him. "Yeah, I punched the guy out."

They all laughed and patted each other on the shoulder and

thighs. Basil couldn't figure out if it was really funny or if it was the fact that Humberto had said it.

"Well, guys, I guess we're finished here," said Carlos. "Now we got to go home and batten down our houses. You okay, Basil," said Carlos.

"I'm okay," said Basil.

"We'll see you later," said Carlos. They all got up, punched him on the shoulder, and walked across the lawn to the parking lot. Carlos looked back at him, waved, and shook his head. Humberto and Ramon nodded in agreement.

Basil figured they were talking about him, laughing at him, or worse, pitying him. Poor man, they were probably thinking, his wife was a witch and his son was gay, no wonder he was always trying to make others laugh. He threw the patties into the lake beside the dead rat.

Picking up his cooler, he looked at it in disgust and dumped it in a garbage can beside the parking lot. He wanted nothing to do with rats. He'd been terrified of them since he was a boy and awoke one night to find a rat nibbling on his toe. He had screamed and the rat had fled, but from then on he always slept with a light on.

Basil walked back to the phones and dialed home. It was Julian who picked up the phone.

"Dad," he said.

"Put your mother on the phone," said Basil.

Sheila came from the garage where she had been stacking up hamster cages. The elementary school where she worked as a teaching assistant had been declared an emergency evacuation site, and no animals were allowed to remain on the premises. She had brought them home as a favour for the principal.

"Tell your son he's staying in the garage!"

"But, honey, I've just put some hamsters down there. The place is really musty."

"You bring rats into my house now!"

"They aren't rats, they're hamsters."

"Rat is rat. I don't want them in my house when I get home."

"I can't do that, honey. I've already promised to take care of them."

Basil hung up the phone. *Great, just great, I'm sharing my house with rats and faggots.*

He got into his pickup and put his toolbox in the back. As he turned out of the parking lot, the wind rushed through the Australian pines that surrounded the soccer fields. So many afternoons he had brought Julian here, teaching him how to kick a football the right way, using the instep instead of the toe. And over on the baseball diamond, although he didn't understand the game – he figured it was like cricket – he taught him to keep his eye on the ball and swing through it. He had even taken him on a fishing trip to the Everglades with all his friends. And for what? For him to turn around and disgrace him like this?

How could he have done this to him after they had sacrificed so much? They had moved from Jamaica to get him out of bad company, struggled to make a life in America and now they finally had a home and two jobs. And what if, after all that, the boy with his little faggot friends contracted AIDS? He turned south on Biscayne Boulevard. He didn't want to think about it.

Miami was beginning to look like a ghost town. All the stores were boarded up against the storm and looters. The few cars that were on the streets were those of last minute shoppers searching for supplies. Pickups laden with plywood, wire and slabs of drywall passed him at the intersection of Biscayne and 125th Street. Basil snickered to himself. He'd done all of his work the night before. He was ready for the storm.

Then he remembered the glass window in the garage hadn't been secured. He was supposed to have brought plywood from the campus, but by the time he got there, Carlos had already doled out the extra pieces to his friends. What was left had to be used on the campus.

It was too late to get anything now. The hardware stores

were probably filled with unprepared people who were being overcharged for simple items. He wasn't going to pay more than he should anyway, and there was nothing of real value in the garage. Julian, his friend, and the hamsters could stay there.

He turned down the avenue where he lived and into the driveway of his house. He parked his pickup between his house and the hedge of his next door neighbour, Marie Boyer. She had been living with her mother, Madam Boyer, since her divorce and the death of her father. Marie had taken the death of her father badly, and Madam Boyer even worse, for she now wandered through the house dressed in black. Basil had been doing all sorts of odd jobs for Marie, cutting the grass and trimming the hedges, and once, while he was clearing the crawl space under the house, she had kissed him. If it hadn't been for Marie's hesitancy, for Marie lived by her mother's word, they would have been together already. If Madam Boyer disapproved of anything – the color of a dress or shade of her shoes – she would change it.

And now the hurricane ruined everything. But it wasn't that Basil no longer loved Sheila. He and Marie had been drawn to each other out of sheer desperation and loneliness. Sheila had changed so much since he had thrown Julian out of the house. She had become such a nag.

The windows of Madam Boyer's house hadn't been covered. Although he told Madam Boyer he could have done the job, she said she didn't want to be a bother, and that she had already hired some men to come and install the hurricane shutters. The men hadn't showed up yet.

He opened the glove compartment, took out a package of condoms he'd bought for his rendezvous with Marie, and slipped them into his pocket. He would hide them later. Sheila was always going though the glove compartment, so he kept them in the tool shed with his power tools. He took his tool box out of the back of the pickup and walked around to the back of the house. The window in the garage could probably be protected by the tool shed, he thought. He checked that the anchoring cables on the tool shed were secure, padlocked the shed and went around to the front.

Julian greeted him as he entered the house.

"Hi, Dad," he said.

"Get back to the garage. I don't want to see you. Just because you're here doesn't mean a thing," said Basil.

The boy's face went blank, and he walked back to the garage. As he closed the door, Basil saw Julian's friend, Gavin, on the cot Sheila had prepared. Behind him were the cages with the hamsters and a rectangular cooler filed with bags of ice. Basil shuddered when he saw the cages. He took bottle of Appleton from the bar he'd built in the living room, poured himself a drink, and walked to the bedroom. Sheila was sitting on her side of the bed.

"It looks like it's going to hit us," said Sheila as she stared at the television.

"Hmm," he mumbled as he pulled the laces of his shoes and kicked them into a corner where a night light still burned.

"It's going to hit somewhere along the South Florida coastline. They haven't figured out the exact landfall, but it will be here by about two or three o'clock tomorrow morning," she said.

"Well, I'm ready," said Basil.

He wanted to forget the storm, the hamsters, and the sight of his son and Gavin. They looked so natural together in their jeans and T-shirts. Nothing like how they looked in the picture. Today they almost looked normal.

But who knows what they were doing downstairs in his garage. What kind of unnatural acts were they performing? He took another sip of his drink and tried not to think about it. Propping a pillow behind his back, he finally found a comfortable position. The doorbell rang.

"I'll get it," said Sheila.

It was just as well, for he wasn't going to get up for anyone now. He was tired. He was going to stay in bed with his bottle of Appleton and ride out the hurricane. He poured himself another drink and listened to the reporter drone on about coordinates and live reports from around the county. A reporter on the beach, a young black man in his early twenties, was interviewing some old people who had ignored the evacuation order and stayed to protect their homes and valuables. There were some kids behind them, wind-surfing fanatics, who sputtered into the microphone, "Waves are awesome!"

There was a knock on the bedroom door and he sprang up. It was Sheila with Madam Boyer.

"She got worried. The workmen haven't showed up. The traffic is really bad, so Marie is staying with her sister in South Dade. She's wondering if she can stay with us. We're not using Julian's old room, so I told her she could stay with us."

"Sure, sure," said Basil.

"You sure, I'm not being a bother," said Madam Boyer.

"No, no bother at all, Madam Boyer," said Basil.

Sheila helped her to Julian's room. The old lady thanked her, seeming almost embarrassed to be there.

When she got back to the room, Basil had gone back to the kitchen for more ice. He didn't want to open the fridge again, for now that he knew the hurricane was definitely going to hit them, he wanted to keep everything as cold as possible. But he also wanted to find out what was happening in the garage. He stood by the door and listened to his son's conversation with Gavin.

"So the three boys find the five dollars and they can't decide what to do with it," said Julian. "They can't buy a toy because they'll fight over it. They can't buy candy because it will spoil their dinner and their moms will get upset. They don't know what to do with the five dollars. Finally, the youngest kid says, 'Let's buy a box of tampons.' 'Tampons,' the other kids say. 'Why tampons?' 'Because,' says the youngest kid, 'on the commercial it says with tampons you can go fishing, biking, running, dancing, all the things you thought you couldn't do'."

The two of them were laughing when Basil opened the door. He had taught Julian that joke before he found out he was gay. Gavin and Julian were facing each other when Basil bent over to get the ice out of the cooler. They continued laughing and Gavin's hand brushed against Julian's leg. Basil exploded.

"What the hell? What the hell is this? I didn't invite you two into my house to go on with that kind of business."

"What, Dad? What kind of business?"

"You think I didn't see that. You think I didn't see that. I saw how he touched you on your leg."

"O please," said Gavin. "I don't need this."

"O please yourself," said Basil. "I saw you."

"I know where I'm not wanted," said Gavin and he walked over to his suitcase and began packing.

"What's going on here?" interrupted Sheila.

"Batty boyism," said Basil. "Batty boyism in my house!"

"That's not true," said Julian. "That's not true. Gavin's my good friend who helped me when you threw me out. I'm just returning the favour. He's the straightest guy in Miami!"

"In Miami that doesn't mean a thing! He still looks kinda bent to me," said Basil, and he picked up the ice and went back to his room.

"I'm leaving," said Gavin.

"No, you're not," said Sheila. "I'm not your mother, but I know what you did for Julian. You're staying here. You can't go out in this weather. The hurricane is due to hit us soon. Let's just see if we can stay here without killing each other."

"But he insulted my friend," said Julian.

"I apologize for your father," said Sheila.

"You've done that too many times, Mom," said Julian.

"Don't say that. Don't let me have to remind you that he's still your father."

"Yes, Mom. I'm sorry," said Julian.

"Now, you boys take care of yourselves," said Sheila. "And, Julian, you lock this door. I'll make sure your father doesn't come down here."

"Yes, Mom, I'll to get a few books from my old room. I'll be right back."

Sheila went with him and knocked on the door. Madam Boyer opened the door.

"Madam Boyer, this is my son, Julian," said Sheila.

"Pleased to meet you," said Madam Boyer.

"I've just come to get a few books," said Julian.

"Is this your room, young man," she said.

"It used to be," said Julian.

"Judging by these books you must be a very intelligent young man," said Madam Boyer. I see *A La Recherche du Temps Perdu*. Parlez vous Francais?"

"Oui," said Julian.

"I'll leave you two alone," said Sheila. As she went back to her room she heard Madam Boyer say, "I heard a lot of shouting and words. You know I am from Haiti, I don't understand a lot of English. I don't mean to pry, but what is a batty boy?"

"It's a long story," said Julian.

"We have all night," said Madam Boyer.

Sheila entered the bedroom and went back to her side of the bed. She continued watching the television and plotting coordinates until Basil fell asleep.

She watched the reports for six hours and her eyes were bleary. Then the screen went blank.

"I guess it's here," she said and nudged Basil. He was snoring.

"Wha? Wha?" said Basil.

"Andrew is here," said Sheila.

They walked out into the living room. There was another power surge and the central air conditioner gave a low moan. Basil turned it off. He looked through the window and saw the oak and avocado trees bending back and forth. Power lines snapped. Branches from their mango tree were broken by the wind and thrown across the street like twigs. On the other side of the street, a piece of aluminium, picked up by the breeze, slammed into the Madam Boyer's window.

Splintered glass flew everywhere.

The next door neighbour's satellite dish was tumbled off its pedestal and frisbeed across the yard. The hurricane was blowing in from the sea and moving fast.

Basil was still tired and a bit tipsy, so he went back to the bedroom. Sheila sat in the living room and was joined by Madam Boyer and Julian, who had waited until Basil had gone.

The storm moved quickly across the county. The lights were out, but the telephones still worked. They were all ready to go outside when there was a sudden gust of wind, the tail end of the hurricane. They heard cables snapping and the sound of metal crashing though glass.

"Help! Help!" screamed Gavin.

They rushed to the garage and saw Gavin buried under the cages and pieces of the tool shed that had crashed through the window.

"Help!" cried Sheila. "Help!"

Basil heard her scream and ran from his room. He stood by the door of the garage and saw them trying to get to Gavin. He tried to join them, but he couldn't move. The hamsters were everywhere.

"Come down and help us," said Sheila.

"Help us, Dad," said Julian as they tried to lift the cages and the suitcases off Gavin's body.

"Don't move him. I'll go call 911," said Madam Boyer as she hobbled past Basil. She went to the living room and dialed the emergency. By the time she came back, Sheila and Julian had already cleared the cages away.

"The paramedics will soon be here," she said. "I told them it was my husband."

Embarrassed and feeling useless, Basil went back to his room. Sheila went to the bathroom and gathered all the towels. She wrapped them around Gavin and held him to her bosom while she waited for the ambulance to arrive.

Sheila, Madam Boyer, and Julian waited with Gavin for four hours and they watched the gray morning light cover the city before there was a knock on the door.

The paramedics went to work immediately. They bandaged Gavin's head and shoulder and carried him up to the living room. Basil stood by the door and watched the proceedings.

"It's a mild concussion," said the chief paramedic. "But you did the right thing by not moving him. It could have been a paralysing injury. So where's your husband?" he said to Madam Boyer.

"As soon as he's well enough, he'll be my husband," said Madam Boyer pointing to Gavin.

The paramedic smiled. He was used to these white lies. Senior citizens always lied about the age of victims because they thought they'd get a quicker response. He looked over the beams of wood and the cages.

"If you guys hadn't cleared away the stuff though, he could have broken his back. You're lucky you had two strong men here," said the paramedic.

"Just one," said Madam Boyer.

"Okay, I'll be going now," said the paramedic. He sensed the tension in the air. He loaded up his medicine chest, took off his gloves and got into the ambulance.

"Is he okay?" Basil asked.

"Yes," said Sheila.

"I'll be going now," said Madam Boyer.

"I'll help you to the door," said Basil.

"No, thanks," said Madam Boyer and grabbed Julian by the arm. "Walk with me," she said. "You're a very interesting young man."

Basil watched Julian and Madam Boyer cross the street.

Over the broken tops of the trees, the gray clouds blotted out the sun. The streets were littered with branches, metal, and glass. All that rubbish, he thought. He walked from the yard, into the intersection and saw all the downed power lines. It would take months before everything was cleared up. The city would never be the same.

Basil walked back to the house, entered the living room and touched his son on his head.

"I'm going for a drink," he said, and went to the kitchen. He peeked into the garage. The hamsters weren't moving. He reached down and picked up Julian's suitcase and saw a picture of their fishing trip in the Everglades, and the look of pride he had on his face when Julian had caught his first fish. Reaching inside his pocket, he looked around, and slipped the pack of condoms into the folds of the suitcase. It was the least he could do.

"Heh, heh, heh, this sucks," said Hector Cueto as he tried to do his best imitation of Beavis and Butthead. He had finished cleaning the graffiti off the classroom which he and his friend, Jorge, had scrawled the day before. *Nigger James*. He handed the bucket of water and the Ajax to the janitor, Mr. Castro, and rejoined the class.

Nigel James, their homeroom teacher, waited for him to take his seat before he opened the letter from the United Way. He already knew the contents of the letter, but he was determined to give the class his speech. He picked up his grade rolls and rearranged the picture of his wife and his one year old daughter.

"Now I know," he said, "that many of you gave to this charity because you knew the winners would get a party in the cafe-teria. But you should have given to help those who are less fortunate than yourselves."

"Here we go again," whispered Hector. "You have to..."

"Something to tell us, Mr. Cueto?" asked Nigel.

"No, no, nothing, Mr. James," said Hector. "Go on with your speech."

"As I was saying," said Nigel, and he continued as if he had not been interrupted, "it's like I haven't taught you anything. It's like I'm not getting through to you. You ninth graders are old enough to understand that you should give without expecting anything in return. You should always give from the heart," and he put his hand over his chest.

Hector rose from his chair, looked around the room, and returned a salute from his chest, Nazi-style.

"From the heart, Mr. James," said Hector.

"Mr. Cueto," said Nigel, "one more outburst like that and I'm sending you down to see Dr. Cabrera and you'll also miss our party."

Hector sat down and kicked the chair in front of him. Jorge Bayardo, his friend and sidekick, awakened from a deep sleep, rubbed his eyes, and rested his head on the desk.

Nigel picked up his ornate letter opener and slit the envelope down the side. The letter opener was a Christmas present from Giselle, his best student in the class. He smiled with her as he opened the letter.

Giselle was part of the new wave of Cuban immigrants and she stood out from the rest of the class not merely because she was smart, but because she was also much darker than the rest of the students. It was Giselle who had stayed after school so many times, despite her father's protests (of which Nigel had no knowledge) and helped him to count the receipts and cash for the charity drive.

Nigel read the letter slowly, then folded it and walked over to the banner he and Giselle had painted for Family Week. *We're all in this together. We can beat Child Abuse.* The second half of the banner was Giselle's idea. He was continually amazed by her verbal abilities. Although she had been in the country for only a year, she seemed to have an innate ability to turn a phrase.

"Well, guys, it seems as if we've won that party and the trip to Disney World. Congratulations!"

"Great," said Hector and the class burst into cheers.

"Yeah, yeah," said Jorge.

The kids were jumping up and down between the rows, hugging and kissing each other. Giselle took a few pictures for her scrapbook. Hector got up and tried to congratulate as many girls he could on the wonderful job they'd done. He gave an extra congratulatory kiss to Giselle. He kissed her on the lips. Nigel was about to reprimand him when Dr. Cabrera opened the door. The children ran back to their seats. Dr. Cabrera was always checking in to see if Nigel was violating any county policies. At first, he thought Dr. Cabrera's prejudice was rooted in something as silly as the fact that he was black, but it was deeper than that.

"Mr. James, may I see you outside," said Dr. Cabrera.

The class hushed as Hector whipped his fingers and some girls giggled. Nigel felt like risking it all and slapping Hector over the head, for if there was ever a case for bringing back corporal punishment, Hector was the best reason.

He walked down the rows of desks he'd arranged with Giselle that morning, and inspected the multi-media learning pod she'd helped him to set up. Above the pods were posters of Shakespeare, Albert Einstein, Beethoven, Stephen Hawking, and a banner, *With Recycling We Can Save The World!* Nigel had read about the learning pods in an issue of *Mensa,* and although he wasn't a member, he always liked to read the articles that had to do with innovative teaching methods. He had won many county, state, and national awards for some of the projects he had done with his students, but he had never been nominated by the staff or Dr. Cabrera for any Teacher of the Year awards.

Closing the door behind him, he stepped outside the classroom, but stood by the rectangular glass window in the centre of the door. He kept his foot in the threshold so he could talk to Dr. Cabrera and observe the class. If anything went wrong, he didn't want anyone to say he'd left the class unattended.

"Mr. James," said Dr. Cabrera. "This is the second time this month, I've had to come to your class to quiet a disturbance."

"With all due respect, Dr. Cabrera, " said Nigel, "this could hardly be called a disturbance."

"So what do you call that commotion I heard from down the hall. This is not the kind of school I run, Mr. James."

"But Dr. Cabrera," pleaded Nigel, "the kids just won the party for the United Way. They contributed more cans of food and money than any other class in the school and in our section of the county."

"I know that," he snapped. "But that's no reason for all the noise. What if the superintendent came by? We'd be in a lot of trouble for failing to keep our students in order."

"Yes, Dr. Cabrera," said Nigel. Once Dr. Cabrera invoked the word "superintendent" all protest ceased.

"I'll see that it won't happen again," said Nigel.

"It better not," said Dr. Cabrera sternly "or we'll be in my office with Mr. Palmer to write a formal complaint, which goes on your permanent record."

"Yes, Dr. Cabrera." And that was it. He wouldn't take it any further. Dr. Cabrera was only too ready to write him up for insubordination, and Nigel knew he was lining up his job for one of his friends. Dr. Cabrera was one of the original members of the Cuban flight in the Sixties, and had scraped his way up to becoming the principal of this school in West Hialeah. He guarded his position ferociously and gave extra assignments to teachers who obeyed him without question, or who gave him information about what was being said about him in the staff lounge. Dr. Cabrera had his favourites, and Mr. Suarez, who had been a political prisoner in Cuba, was ready to take over Nigel's job as the yearbook supervisor. The job paid an extra five thousand dollars a year, and Nigel needed every extra cent he could earn because his wife had gone back to school to study for her bachelor's degree. They wanted to save enough to buy a house and settle down in North Miami and move out of the apartment where they were now living. The area had been a predominantly Anglo area until the Cubans moved in and prompted white flight.

The job at Westchester Middle School wasn't his first choice for the staff were predominantly Cuban, and he would have preferred to have worked in Alapattah or another predominantly black area where he'd have felt more at home. But the school had needed to recruit him as one of the few black English teachers in the county, so that it would comply with court-mandated ethnic ratios, and he had a wife, child, and mortgage to consider.

But now Nigel was in trouble with Dr. Cabrera. Nigel had crossed him when he had caught him out in fixing the photography contract for the school yearbook for a friend. He had thought about exposing Dr. Cabrera to the school board, but decided against it. He thought his act of generosity would put him on Dr. Cabrera's side. He was wrong.

"Well, if you'll excuse me," said Nigel as he looked through the window and saw Hector Cueto playing with his zipper in front of the class, "I think I better get back to my class before they think I've disappeared."

Dr. Cabrera turned, marched down the hallway, and waved to the Union steward, Mrs. Morales.

"Sit down, Hector," said Nigel, "and zip up your pants. There's nothing there that will impress anyone."

"That's what you think. Or do you think your Jamaican bamboo can match the Cuban culebra?" he said sarcastically, trying to imitate Nigel's accent.

He let it pass for he knew it would lead to more teasing, and this was not exactly a topic he should be discussing with a child. His accent was just one more of the things that separated him from his students and the rest of the school.

"Sit down," he said and tried to think of some punishment that could be meted out to Hector.

But Hector was past any punishment he could give him. He served detentions gleefully for it meant he could stay late with his friends on the football team. Nigel had resorted once to giving him lines, "Persistent Perversity Provokes the Patient Pedagogue," even though he knew it was against school board policy, but he was at his wit's end. He told Hector to write the lines one thousand times. Hector turned them in at lunch the same day. They were written in blue, black, green, and purple ink, and a variety of handwritten styles. Nigel figured Hector had his girlfriends write them for him. But who? And what could they possibly see in Hector?

"Someone did these for you," he had said. "You were supposed to do this yourself. No one should have done them for you. Now who did this for you?"

"My cousins."

"You don't have any cousins in this school."

"You don't understand, do you? Around here we stick up for each other. We're all cousins. I'll be here until I graduate. And you can't do anything to stop me."

Nigel was steadily building his case against Hector and with one more referral for disruptive behaviour, he might be heading for an opportunity school. Nigel had documented all the information necessary to convince the bureaucrats who ran the system, but Dr. Cabrera had told him to withdraw the referral. He didn't want it on the record that any of the children from his school could be judged as failures.

"All of our children are redeemable," said Dr. Cabrera, chiding Nigel when he turned in the final papers on Hector. Nigel walked out of the office. There was still the possibility of a recommendation from the school guidance counsellor, Mr. Rodriguez, and Hector would be out of his class. Mr. Rodriguez assured him he would have a reply soon. Soon.

So Nigel let Hector continue with his antics. As long as Hector didn't hurt anyone, and he couldn't be held criminally liable, it was fine. He wasn't going to allow the boy to cost him his job.

Hector looked at him and sailed a paper plane across the classroom. The plane landed on Giselle's desk. She put her hand up and signalled to Nigel.

"Yes, you may go, Giselle," he said as he took a hall pass from his desk. "You'd better take this. Dr. Cabrera is on the warpath."

Giselle nodded, covered her mouth and took the pass that he had made for her. She told him that she had lost the first one, but soon after Hector had been found in the bathroom smoking cigarettes inside the stalls and he had her pass stuck in the front of his cap. Nigel figured he must have stolen it from Giselle. That was the only possible explanation.

"This is against school policy," said Mr. Palmer, who had covered for him. "You've got to stop breaking the rules and doing things that are so unorthodox. Stuff like this will get you in trouble with Attila the Cuban."

"I don't know how to do things differently," said Nigel.

"Well, you better find out and quick or you'll be out on your ass faster than you can say Mariel."

Palmer liked Nigel's rebellious spirit and had gotten him out of trouble many times. He too had worked and struggled from nothing until he'd gained his current position. He had served in the army during WWII, educated himself on the GI bill and had worked up from softball coach to assistant principal. Since Dr. Cabrera's arrival, however, his power had been cut. He had descended from class scheduling to cafeteria control. He now dedicated himself to foiling Dr. Cabrera's plans, though with decreasing energy as each academic year drew to a close. He was just biding his time until retirement. Then he would sell his house in West Hialeah and move to a condo in Broward county away from Miami and all its race wars.

Nigel knew that Palmer was right about his breaking the rules. But what else could he to do to help her? Giselle had gotten herself pregnant and she needed the hall passes almost daily so she could go to the bathroom and throw up. So he gave her another permanent pass and told her to guard it with her life. If anyone found out, he would be in a lot of trouble.

She took the pass from him and held his fingers tightly, to his embarrassment. She had held his hand the same way when she helped him take his books from the back of his brother-in-law's car. His car had been in the repair shop and his brother-in-law, Erwin, had taken him to work. Erwin had taken one look at her curly hair, mocha-brown skin and said, "Nigel, I don't know how you can work here with all these young girls running around. I'd go crazy. I'd have to get a piece."

"Erwin," he said, "these are children. My God, she's only in ninth grade."

"Hey, old enough to bleed..."

"Get out of here, Erwin," he said.

"Can't you see that little girl loves you? Are you blind?"

"I'm just her English teacher who encourages her to develop her mind," he said, and pushed down the latch on Erwin's door.

"You worship her mind and I'll worship her body."

But Erwin had merely confirmed what he had long suspected: Giselle had a schoolgirl crush on him. He also had to admit that he was flattered she had taken an interest in him. He had been drawn to her after hearing the children call her 'Spic Nigger'. He knew what it felt like to be the only black person in an all Hispanic school. The colour of her skin made her different from the other Cubans and her culture from the few African-American students in the school. She was not welcome in either group, so she had gravitated towards him, the other outsider.

And now she'd gotten herself pregnant. How could a girl as smart as Giselle allow this to happen? He didn't know, but he was determined she would not end up like so many girls he had known in Jamaica, their lives over at fifteen because of an unwanted child.

"Now come back quickly," he said.

"Teacher's pet," shouted Hector as she walked out the door.

"Hector, why do you like to give so much trouble?"

"It's not trouble, Mr. James," said Hector dropping into a tone of mock humility. "It's just that it's not fair that she can go to the bathroom when the rest of us can't. What makes her so special?"

"Giselle," said Nigel defensively, "is one of the brightest

students in this class. I'd say she was even one of the most intelligent persons I've ever met,"

"Whooooooooo," went the class.

"Come on, guys. You know what I mean."

"What do you mean?" asked Hector.

"She's in honours science, math, English, French and Spanish. She was the editor of the school newspaper and she's going to be an assistant editor of the school yearbook next year. She could teach you a lot about being a good student."

"I bet she could," said Hector with a smile. "But that doesn't explain why she can go to the bathroom when the rest of us can't."

"Well, let's say girls are different," said Nigel.

"I know," said Hector, with the same twisted smile.

The bell rang and they all rushed through the door and formed a line. Hector woke up Jorge.

"If this line isn't formed properly, and if there's any talking or screaming in the hallway," said Nigel sternly, "we'll all come back to the classroom and no one will go to this party. Am I making myself clear, Hector?"

"Yes, Mr. James," said Hector.

"Okay," said Nigel. "Let's form a neat line and make sure we don't disturb anyone else."

As they moved away from the door, Jorge squealed and pulled a piece of paper from his back. Hector had hit him because he had a sign on his back that said, "*Soy un maricon como Mr. James. Mata me!*"

"What's going on?" asked Nigel. "Do you want us to turn back right here?"

"We were just playing," said Hector. "Weren't we, Jorge?"

"Yeah, yeah," said Jorge as he rubbed the back of his neck.

The line snaked down the hallway. On the way they passed Mr. Palmer's who, when Nigel smiled at him, grimaced and turned away. Probably indigestion. He'd talk with him later. As they passed the girls' bathroom, Giselle came out.

"Are you okay?"

"Yes," said Giselle as she joined the line quickly.

The line looped around the science department and through the double doors to the computer department. Everything was planned. His substitute teacher, Mrs. Martinez, was there. He would take Giselle, without his wife's knowledge, to the family's gynaecologist. He had told the doctor she was his niece and that she'd gotten into trouble. The doctor had sympathized and agreed to perform the operation.

As they walked towards the cafeteria, Nigel weighed his options and figured he was doing the right thing.

She had told him her father would kill her if he found out, and her mother never protected her from him. She would have to drop out of school to take care of the baby because her parents were Catholic and they didn't believe in abortion. He couldn't allow this to happen to her. It was too much of a waste of a life that could be productive and useful. He couldn't sit back and do nothing. He would save her.

They entered the cafeteria and the music boomed out of the speakers located behind the cashiers. They were playing a song that Dr. Cabrera had banned, but the kids ignored him and played it anyway, *"Mama, que sera lo quiere el negro?"*

Giselle grabbed his hand and invited him to dance.

"No, no," he said.

"Come on, Mr. James," she said. "Let's dance!"

"Dance, dance, Mr. James," shouted Hector. "Hey, everybody, look, Mr. James is dancing!" Hector pulled the camera away from Giselle and took a picture of them standing beside each other.

"Dance, dance," they all screamed, and he finally gave in and danced to *"Mama, que sera lo quiere el negro?"*

After they finished dancing, Nigel signaled her to meet him at the furthest end of the school parking lot. Giselle went first and he walked over to the cashiers. Mrs. Martinez was talking in Spanish with one of the cashiers.

"I'll be back at twelve," he said. "The lesson plans are on my desk."

"Yes." she said and continued talking with the cashier.

He slipped out by the back of the cafeteria. Giselle was waiting for him beside his car. As he walked towards her, three policemen walked up to him and grabbed him. Ray Santiago, a reporter from a local television station that featured sensational scoops of arrests, and DEA shoot-outs with cocaine kingpins, stuck a microphone in his face. An HRS official and a member of the school board watched as the police handcuffed him.

"What, what have I done?" he asked.

"Don't be coy, Mr. James," said Dr. Cabrera. "We know what happened between you and the girl. She told us everything. You should be ashamed of yourself. And a married man at that. What are you going to tell your children? Child molester!"

"Child molester?" he said.

"Yeah, contributing to the delinquency of a minor, buddy. Oh, they'll just love your ass in the county jail," said one of policemen.

"Why? Why, Giselle?" he asked as they held him in front of the cameras. The entire class had left the cafeteria and were watching him as he was interrogated by Ray Santiago.

"Why did you do this to me Giselle?" he asked again.

Hector burrowed through the crowd and smiled when he saw the police leading him away.

"You taught her well, Mr. James. She did as you taught her, from the heart," said Hector as he wrapped his arm around Giselle's stomach and she held his hand.

"From, from the heart?" stuttered Nigel.

"From the heart," said Hector.

"Yeah, yeah," said Jorge.

THE DUPPY IN LIMBO

Things was slow at the Limbo Lounge. Me and Jacko was sitting inside the restaurant, when the mad woman who used to kotch outside the gate at the crossroads get up an say, "This place too raas quiet! It too dead. Me a go down to one nine-night that livelier than this place." That's when Jacko, the hotel guide, start one heap a cursing and bad word in the yard.

"Galang, you old battle axe, galang. Look pan you. You foot back rusty like crab batty." Jacko always say that was the problem with Jamaica today – the woman them was too liberated, too extra, and too damn out-of-order.

"Think bout it," he said to Mr. Nelson, the manager, "think bout it. Even mad woman can pass judgment in dis island. When me was a boy, when Captain Crichlow used to ride on him horse through this copse, not a soul, not even a army of man could stand up to him. And you can bet that when him was alive, that mad woman couldn' spend even a half hour outside him gate."

But that's Jacko. Him always talking about the old time days with Captain Crichlow, the old Englishman who, when Jacko deep under him waters, him call 'Captain Crutchlow' and 'Captain Crutchbox'. And him always telling him old time sayings like, "Man who born to hang cyaan drown", that nobody can figure out up to now.

But if the mad woman leave, the hotel would really be empty. If it wasn't for the one guest, Miss JA from Miami, who was living in the special guest cottage, all of us would be at home on top of Mt. Airy. She one was a headache, but we had to put up with it, for Mr. Nelson was depending on her to carry some good news about the hotel back to Miami. I think she did like Mr. Nelson and was hoping to get a *real* island welcome. I know Mr. Nelson did want to help her. Everybody on the compound know that even though Mr. Nelson married, him have a taste for tourist meat. Jacko used to help him set up a few tourist, for as Jacko say, a man cyaan just eat fowl, fowl, fowl every day. Some day a man just feel for beef.

But today Mr. Nelson had a whole heap of things on him mind. Him was worried that him father, the owner, was coming down that night from Kingston to the hotel and it was empty. Him did already tell Mr. Nelson that him was going sell the hotel if business wasn't good. Mrs. Nelson was coming with him, and she was all for selling the hotel for she never like the idea of her husband being all the way down in Negril on his own. She hear some rumours that Mr. Nelson was giving a warm Jamaica welcome to all the female guests and she never like it. She could never prove it, but she never like it.

She was dead set against the hotel from it open. She say it was too out-of-the-way, and that it would take all kind of gimmicks to make the tourists come all the way down there for things they could get in Negril self. But that's what Mr. Nelson say him wanted the Blue Moon to be – a quiet place where tourist could come and rest, away from the noise and bustle of Negril. And it was true, the place was quiet, but the tourists wanted more, and now it was too quiet and too late to change things. So when Jacko go tell him that the mad woman was really leaving, him wave Jacko away for the mad woman was the least of him worries.

But Jacko did know better. Him did remember the long speech Mrs. Nelson did give we about the mad woman. One day she see the two of we taunting her, and Mrs. Nelson, who only stay at home and sometimes help in the Family Court in Kingston, say that we should stop abusing her. She say that woman was the backbone of the island, and how we should respect woman. Mrs. Nelsone say that everytime she come to the hotel she want to see the mad woman, and that the mad woman could stay by the gate as long as she want. Jacko object because him did want to get rid of her from long time.

Is then Mrs. Nelson give me the job to make sure that the mad woman get breakfast and dinner every day. It wasn't no big thing for she wasn't a dirty mad woman. She keep herself nice and clean for she used to bathe every day down by the seaside behind the rocks. Sometimes, too, she can talk normal for days, but then she will go on for a whole month talking to herself and cursing bad words. One day I ask Jacko if him know what drive her mad. Him say the reason she stay by the cross roads is because she waiting for her secret boyfriend who promise him would meet her there, but who never show up. That's what drive her mad.

We couldn't stop her from going though. We even tried to coax her with a Dragon and a spliff, for she used to roll three big head and smoke them one after the other, but today she was low.

"No, I want two Dragon and two spliff and no bush either. I want the good sensi," she said.

"Make the mad woman galang," said Jacko. "Me nah give her no Dragon. She can guwane bout her business."

But when she left, our last entertainment was gone. We was soon tired of playing dominoes and Ludo. When the mad woman was there we had a whole heap of fun.

If Jacko was feeling generous him would buy her a Dragon and give her a spliff. One day she get drunk and she turn her back to us, throw up her frock over her head and say, "Me is Nanny, Queen of the Maroons. Shoot at me, throw all the rock you want, but if I catch one in my back side, I will fire it back at you the same way I kill off the English."

I was going throw a rockstone at her but Jacko line say, "Peradventure, you lick her with the stone and she dead. You

106

can go court house for mad woman. Then suppose you lick her real hard, and she come fe lick you, wha you guwane do? A mad woman ever lick you? It no nice. De two worse summady fe lick yu is a mad man or a drunkard. Them don't have no feeling. And now she mad and drunk!"

So we had nothing else to do but sit down inside the restaurant and watch the John Crows circling over Mt. Airy. I had just finished spray painting the grill door to the restaurant, and took my usual spot facing the juke box, and Jacko sit down with him back to the side door so him could look out through the window.

"More than the usual amount of John Crow today," I said to him.

"Rain fall last night," he said. Jacko knew the hills and gullies of Negril like the bumps on his forehead. "A couple a dog probably get lost in the cave and fall down inna the sink-hole. Plenty man and dog dead up inna them hills. Them say that's where Captain Crichlow dead."

"How him dead," I ask.

"Pum-pum kill him," said Jacko. "Cut down in the prime of him life by pum-pum. Never see a man like him for loving a big batty woman. Old time people say anybody who disturb him grave will have more plague than John in the Revelation. Is a serious duppy up in them hills."

If Jacko did know Miss JA was in the restaurant him wouldn' say nothing about duppy, for Miss JA just break inna we conversation the minute she hear the word.

"You mean there are ghosts, what you call duppies, up on Mt. Airy," she say. "Jacko, how come you've never taken me there?"

Jacko false teeth nearly drop out of him mouth, "Where you come from?"

"I was in the pool. I came to order my dinner," she said.

"You never have to do that," said Jacko. "I tell you this morning I will take care of that fa you."

"I also wanted to talk about on going to Mo Bay for the Rosehall Great House. But if we have our own ghost right here, why should I go all the way to Mo Bay?"

"This is just idle talk to frighten the boy," said Jacko, and he winked at me. "Just idle talk ,Miss JA." Miss JA was the name Jacko give her after she pressure him to give her a name. That was Jacko habit. Him give everybody a different name, and then him never change. Him call the manager, Mr. Nelson, 'Wellington' because him was always wearing them; Rupert, the cook, him call 'Dog Head', and me him call, 'MacIntosh'. When Miss JA find out that everybody have a name except her, she start after him. Jacko say that what she really wanted was a good oil job, but him was too old and too blind. Him say Mr. Nelson was out of the question – it was too close to him wife coming down to Negril, and that woman can sense these things.

Him say maybe I should do it. But I see her one day down by the beach, naked as the day she born, and I say no Baba, the woman too pink. And she was really fat. If she did ever roll over on my maga bone, them wouldn't find me till two week later.

But she wouldn' stop until Jacko give her a name: Miss JA. Him tell her that's what they call all the winner of the beauty contest in Jamaica. But him never tell her it was the name of him favourite milking cow that dead a few years back.

But that was the kind of woman she was, once she start something, she never stop. "I don't believe you," she say. "But I'll make it really worth it for you if you take me up into the hills tonight."

The woman was a botheration, but she had money. She had Jacko running all over the island chasing duppies. She drive in the hotel van to Lover's Leap and Struie to see the tomb of the headless horseman. "Never see a woman love duppy so," said Jacko.

Jacko scratched his head and looked up at the hills. When he was a boy, duppies used to chase him and his brother, Ronald, through the copse and down the side of the hill. Even to this day, Ronald refused to get firewood from the copse for fear of duppies, and no matter how Jacko assured him, "Duppy don't walk in daylight," Ronald wouldn't believe him.

"I'll pay you double," she said. "Think about it. Sixty American dollars for fifteen minutes work. That's more than I make!"

Jacko shook his head. "No, ma'am. Me don't take nobody inside them caves after dark. Bad things might happen."

Jacko was too deep in the conversation to notice that Mr. Nelson was in the restaurant, and all the nudge me a nudge him, the stubborn old man just turn him back more to Miss JA.

"Jacko, you mean you're not taking our guest up on her offer?" asked Mr. Nelson.

"Nuff respect, Boss," said Jacko, and turned around for he knew how Mr. Nelson feel about tourist demands. Mr. Nelson would do anything to keep the hotel or even one guest happy. One time, he took Jacko aside when he was beating the tourists in dominoes and said, "Be kind to the tourists" which meant he should let the tourists win most of the games. Now this was something that Jacko never like because that old man could read a domino game better than him could read a book. It used to hurt him to lose on purpose, for in him teenage days him was the best domino player in Negril. The tourists would never know him was letting them win, for he would sabotage him own hand so well, nobody would know. Except me.

At least when the tourist win, they would buy him drinks and drop him a few dollars. Jacko liked that. None of the hotels in Negril would hire him, and working at the Blue Moon was easy money. He wasn't going to spend the rest of his days like his brother, Ronald, up in the hills around goats, chicken and bang belly children.

"Boss, me no really want go up inna them hills after dark. Me cyaan see too well, you know. Me glaucoma and all."

This was only half-true. Jacko was totally blind in his left eye, but he could still see well enough with the right. He could make it through a copse faster than a bush rat without bucking him toe.

"And is murder inside them cave if you don' know you way," said Jacko.

"I wouldn't want to go all the way," said Miss JA . "The mouth of the cave would be fine. Couldn't MacIntosh take me then?"

I could have kill Jacko right then. Now him have this white woman calling me MacIntosh when me real name was Sean.

"That boy couldn't fine him backside in a latrine," Jacko sayd.

"I really want to go there before I leave," said Miss JA. "It would be another dimension to your charming, but quiet, hotel. It would open," she said, and she turn to Mr. Nelson, "another niche in the tourist market. It would be very interresting to tell the other travel agents about this added attraction at your hotel. Your hotel needs something that no other hotel has. As it is now, it has very little to offer."

When Mr. Nelson hear that, him say, "I'll take you there. Jacko draw me a map. Sean, get some paper and you help him. The three of us can go there tonight."

How I get myself in the middle of this, I don't know. I had other things to do. After the rain that did fall last night, me and Mr. Joseph, the owner of another hotel, was going crab hunting. Him was going pay me twenty Jamaican dollar for every crab me catch. Not that him couldn't catch them himself. Dat Chinee man could see and catch crab better than me. I think him did just need more hand to catch the crab. Him could catch crab with the light from a matches. Sometimes, in the middle of the night, after we empty the slot machines at Treetop Hotel, him just pull over to the side of the road, turn off the engine, run out of the car like him mad, and then dig down in the bush and find crab. Jacko call him Joseph "Crab" Chung Fah.

Well, in two-twos, Miss JA run over to her room for her

Ouija board and Mr. Nelson go for him Wellington and a flashlight. I get the paper and a sit down beside Jacko. I start draw the hotel and the back, but Jacko turn to me and say, "I not going help you draw no raas map. Just listen to me, an listen to me good."

Jacko pointed towards the copse and said, "You see that mango tree? When you get there, go ten chains, then turn left at the tamarind tree. Walk three more chains, then turn left. You will see a big stone and that will lead you straight into a small cave. Just take them to the front where it no so dark. Wait about fifteen minutes. By then, you will hear a loud noise that bound to frighten them. But don't worry is the wind from off Mt. Airy and the breeze off the sea coming up through the sinkholes. It used to frighten me. Ronald shit up him pants the first time him hear it. Now you have everything?"

"Yes," I said.

"Then tell me what I tell you," said Jacko.

I repeated the directions, then Jacko get a glass of white rum from behind the bar. He poured some on the ground, took a sip, then rubbed some over my face and over my arms.

"What that for? Mosquito?" I asked.

"No is fa duppy. Now drink the rest," he said. "Dis will protect you. I don't want no duppy settle pon you and take over you body."

I didn't believe him, but I wasn't taking any chances. Still I never want to drink the white rum, for my mother, who is a Christian, always tell me that white rum-drinking was the start of reprobate living. It was drinking, she say, that lead my father to the path of wickedness, fornication and whore-mongering. One day she catch me in the restaurant sipping a rum punch and she walk across and caulk me over me head, right in front of the tourist. I was going cuss her off, and Jacko would have help me too, for Jacko don't take no foolishness from any woman, but Mr. Nelson come in and we had to bite we tongue.

"She did wrong fe lick you in front of the tourist," said Jacko.

"It not right. Woman must know her place. I know she is you mother an everything, but she have to know that you is the king. Plus, she don't know the power of white rum. Sometime, and you listen to me boy, me think it can raise the dead."

That's why I love to hang round Jacko, him always tell the truth. And is not that him hate woman or anything when him talk like that. Jacko, people tell me, was engaged to married with a girl from Sav-la-mar, but she run off with a tourist to Ocho Rios. The man full up her head with foolishness about the good life in America and take her away with him. After him done use her, him give her some bus fare back to Negril. The worse part, though, was that Jacko never know what was going on. She tell him that she was visiting her aunt in Kingston, but she write a letter to Ronald to let him know everything. That's what hurt Jacko so much. Him own brother know more about what was happening with him own woman than him. When she come back, she start beg Jacko to take her back.

"Me no want no brand new second hand gal," said Jacko. Him say, as far as him was concern, she was a dead woman. So Ronald marry her and since she dead, him don't leave the house. Jacko never forgive him.

I take the last sip of my white rum and Miss JA come back with her Ouija board. Mr. Nelson have him flashlight. I take another sip from Jacko glass.

"You remember what I tell you," said Jacko.

"Yes," I said and I repeated the directions.

"All right," said Jacko and the three of we start tramping through the bush to find Miss JA's duppy.

We start out through the back of the compound, and then we reach the mango tree. We walk the ten chains and we turn left at the tamarind tree. By the time we get there, the white rum start to lick me, and me never know which way to go. Miss JA say we should go left, and Mr. Nelson, who agree with anything a tourist say, especially if is a woman, agree with her. But I remember what Jacko say, that woman must know them place, and I tell them that is me Jacko give the directions, so them should follow me. The truth is I never want them to know I couldn't hold my waters.

So we turn right, and although we never see the big stone, we start to go straight and a walkway lead we to the mouth of a big cave. Mr. Nelson turn on him flashlight and we enter the cave. Miss JA pull her Ouija board out of the box. Then the three of we sit in a circle and she start to chant a chant that me couldn' make out the word. Then she put her hand on the pointer and start call on the spirit that was in the caves. Now me, I was just grinning all the way because I was just waiting to hear the sound that would frighten them away and I could go crab hunting.

We sit down there for a good fifteen to twenty minutes and nothing was happening. With all the chant Miss JA was chanting, and with all the spin she was spinning the pointer, nothing was happening. So then she start pull her hair out of the pony tail. Then she start loosen her blouse and start calling to the spirits. She finally pull off her blouse and was down to her bra. Mr. Nelson say, "Please, Miss Jameson, I know our beaches are clothing optional, but you can't do that up here."

But she wouldn't listen and she strip down to her panty and bra. But still nothing happen. We wait five more minutes, and again nothing. Finally Miss JA say, "This was a waste of time. There are no spirits here."

So she start pick up her clothes and I smell something like smoke coming out of the cave. The smoke start come out of the cave and it make my hair stand up on me neck. It circle over me head and around me body, then move fast, like it hear news, away from me and settle on Mr. Nelson.

"Let's get out of here," said Miss JA.

Mr. Nelson nod and then say, "Whey de raas you think you going?"

And Miss JA said, "Excuse me, what did you say?"

"I say, whey de raas you think you going?"

Miss JA get frighten, and when I look in Mr. Nelson eye it was red like fire. She start pick up her clothes and as she bend over to pick up her skirt, Mr. Nelson shout, "Big batty gal! Me love a big batty gal" and him run and grab her from behind. Well, Miss JA never seem to mind, so the two of them start run and chase each other around and pretty soon she and Mr. Nelson was tumbling in the bush. I never want to see that kind of nastiness, for my mother always teach me to walk the straight and narrow path and I was definitely in the shadow of death.

So I start running down the hill and I find my way back to the restaurant. I could hardly explain myself to Jacko when twenty minutes later, Mr. Nelson and Miss JA show up. She was laughing all the way and him was feeling up her bottom.

When them finally get inside the restaurant, Miss JA went back to the poolside to get her towel. Is then Jacko see Mr. Nelson countenance, and say, "Captain, Captain Crichlow, is you dat, sah?"

And Mr. Nelson say, "Jacko, Jacko , is you that? The last time I see you, you was a boy. What happen to you?"

"I get old, Captain. But I see you up to you old tricks. What happen to you?"

"I was trapped up in them hills till this woman release me," and him tickle her bottom again. "It was cold up there till she come and wake me up. What a nice woman, eh? Turn round," he said to Miss JA as she was going up the stairs, "Turn round, turn round." And Miss JA turned to us. "You ever see a nicer batty than this. For a white woman she have a big batty, you know. My wife never have a batty like that!" and him run over to her, feel her bottom and say, "Nice, nice."

We never know what to do. Mr. Nelson was fooling around with Miss JA by the pool and doing all kind of things. Then Mr. Nelson said, "I'm tired of this place. Let's go into Negril."

"But you can't go to Negril, Mr. Nelson," I say.

Him pull me aside so Miss JA couldn' hear and him say, "I

don't name Mr. Nelson. Call me the Captain or I will murder you little raas. You hear me!"

"Yes, sah," I said and him and Miss JA jump into the van.

"Let me go with you," said Jacko, but before him could say another word Miss JA ram the car in first gear and them fly through the gate. So we do the only thing we could do, we start fix up the place before Mr. Nelson wife and father get there.

"We cyaan afford fe lose this hotel," said Jacko. "This duppy going mash up everything. We have to stop the duppy."

"How you stop a duppy?" I ask him.

"Me don't know," said Jacko, "but me will think of something."

We finally finish cleaning the pool when we hear the horn blow and Miss JA and Mr. Nelson arrive with the van full of people. Mr. Nelson and Miss JA start limbo contest, wet T-shirt contest, and all kind of things like what them have at Sandals.

Soon we was serving Red Stripe and white rum. We had to send word up to Mt. Airy to wake up the bartender, Albert, for only him did know how to mix the drinks that the tourists wanted like 'Zombie' and 'Sex on the Beach'.

We even had to send down to Negril for more ice, for the tourists was coming in from all over. Blue Moon was a hit. Word was passing through the town and everybody wanted to come and see what was happening. The bartender send word to him brother who play in a band, and them bring the whole band to the hotel.

Even the Rasta boys was selling spliff outside the gate and getting a lot of tourist high. Everybody was dancing and having a good time. Is then Captain Crichlow pointed to one of the tourist wearing a T-shirt with Hard Rock Cafe on the front and picked up the can of spray paint I'd left under the counter and said, "I name hereso: *The Red Dread Cafe*. From henceforth and into perpetuity it shall be called by that name." And him spray the name over the bar.

Everything was going well, except Captain Crichlow was dancing with another tourist woman. He had worn out Miss JA. She was upstairs by the poolside sleeping on one of the lounge chairs. She couldn't keep up with him. The duppy look like it was going kill off all the people with excitement.

He started with another tourist woman, and the usual "Big batty gal. Me love a big batty gal". Then the phone in the office start to ring. It was Mrs. Nelson. She say she would be at the hotel in one hour.

"Drive me down to Negril," Jacko say.

"Why?" I ask.

"Don't argue with me," he say, and he throw a six-pack of Dragon into the van and the two of us jumped in. Jacko buy three spliffs from the Rastas at the gate and headed down the hill. We drive round and the town till we find the nine-night where the mad woman was. Jacko get out of the van and give her a spliff.

She take it from him, and then him give her a Dragon.

"If you come back to the hotel wid we, I will give you the pack," Jacko say.

"I not coming wid you."

"Why?" asked Jacko

"Because you always annoying me, and after what you say this morning about me foot back, I not going nowhere wid you."

I could see that Jacko was ready to leave, but him open a bottle of Dragon, sip it and cool himself down.

"You know me can finish this pack by myself, you know. You coming or not?" he ask.

"Say you sorry," said the mad woman.

"Wha?" said Jacko.

"Say you sorry and I will come with you."

Jacko took another sip of the Dragon. "All right, I sorry. Now get in the van."

"How I know that when I get in the van you won't take advantage of me?" said the mad woman.

"I look like I would want to have anything to do with you? Besides, the manager wife want you back on the compound," said Jacko. "We have to take care of you."

"So that's why you is here. It going cost you three spliffs then," said the mad woman.

"Anything," said Jacko. "Just get in the van."

So the mad woman agree and she get in the van. We drive up the hill like we mad and turn into the compound where Mr. Nelson was dancing the conga. Him had a tourist woman in front of him and was tickling her bottom the same way.

"If we going keep the hotel, we have to move fast," said Jacko.

Jacko hustled the mad woman into Mr. Nelson room and promise her another six-pack of Dragon if she would bathe and put on one of Mrs. Nelson dress. When the mad woman hear there was more Dragon in store, she run to the room quick-quick, bathe and put on the dress. Jacko reach under the bar inside Mr. Nelson room and give her the six pack of Dragon and she drink one by one and kotch the bottles on top of the dresser with the picture of Mrs. Nelson.

In the meantime, I managed to tear Captain Crichlow away from the conga line. I told him that Jacko had someone special for him in the room. "A real big batty gal". So him hurry with me to the room. When him get there and Jacko show him the mad woman in Mrs. Nelson dress, him wasn't too impressed.

Him was going leave when Jacko say, "Nanny, come forward," and the mad woman, who was drunk by now, fling up her frock in the air and say, "I can catch bullet, rockstone and rocket! Fire away."

And Captain say, "Eunice! Is you that? I would know that backside anywhere!"

And the mad woman say, "Captain! Captain! Is you that? Oh, my Captain, my Captain! You finally show up!"

Captain Crichlow jump on top of the mad woman and the two of them start tear off them clothes. Jacko and me leave the room for we figured them had a whole heap a things to talk about. As Jacko close the door, we see Mrs. Nelson and Mr. Nelson father drive in.

We run down to the office, greet them and take them over to the office. We give them drinks and Mr. Nelson father was happy to see the bar so full. By then Miss JA wake up and walk over to we.

"Great hotel, Jacko. I'm going to tell all the other travel agents in Miami to book all our customers here."

Mr. Nelson father face brighten up, but that didn't impress Mrs. Nelson and she start to ask where her husband was. We tell her that he was taking care of some business, and that he would soon be there. She waited and waited and then after ten minutes, she demand us to show her where her husband was. Jacko tell me to go ahead. Mr. Nelson father said him would follow we, but then him sit down and start talk with Miss JA.

I was walking towards the apartment when I hear, "Lawd, a dead again!" Then silence. I look up at the apartment and I see the mad woman running from the door and down the side of the beach. She was still wearing Mrs. Nelson dress.

Mrs. Nelson run past me and up to the apartment. When she get inside, she see her half-naked husband on the floor, him eye wide and watery like a blowfish.

She run over to him side cover him up and start slap him face.

"Roger, Roger, wake up! Wake up, sweetheart."

Jacko go to the bar, get some white rum, and give it to Mrs. Nelson to wipe him face. She wipe her husband face with the rum and him start to wake up. She give him another slap and him come back to himself.

"What, what's happening," said Mr. Nelson.

"Roger, oh Roger, I though I'd lost you. What did that mad woman do to you?"

Jacko looked at Mr. Nelson and winked, then turned to Mrs. Nelson and said, "You see ma'am, this is what we never want to tell you from long. That mad woman been thiefing you clothes off the clothesline and been telling people that she married to your husband. She is the one who been spreading all them lies about Mr. Nelson and other woman. I did tell him that him shouldn't talk to her alone. But that's what happen when you try to reason with mad people. Him lucky she never kill him."

Mrs. Nelson look at Jacko hard to see if him telling her the truth and Jacko just turn the blind eye towards her. Mr. Nelson never say anything. Him just listen to everything that Jacko say and nod him head as usual. It wasn't the first time Jacko get him out of a hole. Mrs. Nelson thank Jacko and she tell him that she don't want the mad woman near the hotel again.

"I will try me best," said Jacko. "But I cyaan promise you anything. Look what she do to a big strapping man like you husband. Imagine what she would do to an old man like me."

Mrs. Nelson look at Jacko hard. Mr. Nelson thank Jacko, put on him shirt, and walk with we back to the bar. Him order drinks for all of we and everybody was happy. To this day Mr. Nelson don't remember what happen. Jacko say him lucky that Mrs. Nelson revive him or else the two of them, him and Captain Crichlow, would have end up in the same cave.

Since then, Mr. Nelson don't even look at another woman, and Mrs. Nelson living in the guest cottage where she help the poor women from Negril take their baby-fathers to court. Other than that, business is great. People coming from all about to see the caves and the mysterious Captain Crichlow. The mad woman, I hear, gone back to live with her people in Darliston. In the meantime, the reggae band going great at *The Red Dread Cafe* and we selling Red Stripe and Dragon, and enough white rum to drunk off the whole of Negril. Jacko say, though, if business start go bad again, we might have to bring back the Captain to lively up the place. Count me out, I tell him. But Jacko say him have the perfect person for the job: Ronald.

Early morning. Mist settled in the abandoned gully project littered with corrugated zinc, discarded tires and heaps of marl. Scavengers would soon be out, scraping whatever they could from the city's refuse, fighting John Crows and herds of wandering pigs for anything edible under the rubble. The lone sound of a transistor radio bleated beyond the gurgle of the river, coursing its way through the sleeping lives of August Town. Street lights flickered out.

Glen Harding stood by the window staring at the wet brightness of the morning reflected off the asphalt road. He walked over to his favourite chair in a corner of the living room and slumped between the arms; his shirt tails hung limply between his legs. His clothes felt as if they belonged to someone else; his trousers were held up by a piece of cord; even his slippers seemed grotesque. Everything seemed so big, his body so diminished. Not that he'd been overweight before. Five years ago, on his twenty-ninth birthday, Sandra, his wife, had put him on a diet of vegetables and greens. Glen hadn't objected; he should have been a vegetarian anyway, keeping strictly Ital, for he was a Rastaman from the tribe of Naphtali, but could not resist, every now and then, indulging in some curried goat, stewed beef or even jerk chicken. But never jerk pork. He had never slipped that far.

He rose and paced the room. Tall and broad-shouldered with a full beard, his movements betrayed his exhaustion. He tapped himself just below his rib cage.

The tenderness was gone. The doctors had told him this was all to be expected. Matching a liver donor and recipient in the short time they had was a miracle, and with the added trauma of the bullet wounds he'd received, he was lucky to be alive. Lucky to be alive? What did they mean?

He couldn't wait for the morning to come. He'd been waiting three weeks for his friend, Duffus, to return from the States, and he'd gotten word that he was coming to see him that day.

He'd met Duffus when the two of them were going through Brigadista training in Cuba. They had completed their training together and were part of the last unit to be trained in Cuba. They came home to a changed country, and went back to Danny Forbes' posse. Danny Forbes, an inveterate gambler, was the top ranking henchman for the Member of Parliament in the area. At first, it had just been the usual job of protection for the members of their political party, but Duffus had shown real courage when a group of Danny's gambling partners, who suspected him of cheating at poker, lay waited Danny at a dance and tried to ambush them. Duffus, in one motion, shoved Danny with such force that he fell to the ground, then dived on top Glen. He took three shots in his arm, neck and thigh, but still managed to fire off six rounds from his own gun to scare off the attackers who, it turned out, were some inexperienced kids. From then on, Duffus never took any chances.

Across the room, Glen could hear Sandra's breathing. He watched her turning in the bed. His eyes followed her legs up to her narrow waist, delicate shoulders and her thin face, framed by dark-brown hair and eyes so black, he could often see his reflection in them. Sandra shifted and stretched her hands over her head. She was awake.

"Yu up early dis mornin," she said as she searched for her glasses.

"Cudn' sleep las' night. Evry time me head lick de pilla, me start dream de same dream. I doan tink I get a ounce a sleep. So me jus kotch here by de window and watch yu and David. Me tink de col' him have gettin betta."

"Me tink so meself. De tea Miss Prince give him really work good. I guwane put on some hot water to make some fa him dis mornin. Yu want some too, or yu want some coffee?"

"Coffee, dis mornin."

Sandra rose from the bed and stumbled into the kitchen. He watched her as she got up, her breasts just showing through the cotton nightdress. She picked up a toy truck David had left on the floor and turned to Glen.

"Yu still tinking bout wha happen?"

"How yu know?"

"I can always tell, yu always get quiet-like. Glen, believe me yu cudn' do a ting. It was six a dem to two of you. Yu lucky yu get way alive."

Glen put his finger over the wound in his side. Everything had healed; there was no pain. But he was still having trouble in the mornings. Sometimes, he vomited blood. He pulled down his shirt. He knew the sight of his bullet- scarred body made Sandra uneasy.

"I guwane go see if David wake yet while yu mek brekfas," he said.

Glen walked quietly into the room and sat on the side of the bed. He gently rocked the child, but David was fast asleep. Him get dis from him mother, thought Glen. Her family could sleep through a hurricane without waking, whereas one drop of rain on the zinc roof made Glen stir from his bed.

"David, David, wake up."

Glen stroked his son's hair, ran his fingers along his nape and down the front of his shirt.

"David, David, wake up."

The boy rubbed his eyes, yawned, and held out his arms to be hugged. Glen hugged him and kissed him on the forehead. David was a handsome boy who had inherited his mother's good looks and intense eyes. They gleamed with delight at the sight of Glen.

"Mornin, Daddy."

"Mornin, Sah. Yu sleep awright."

"Yes, Daddy."

"So yu reddy to go to school then?"

David frowned, shook his head sideways, and broke into a smile. Glen rubbed his palm over his forehead and they laughed together.

"Yu guwane grow up worthless if yu doan go to school, yu know that? Come and wash yu face, an I we help yu get dress. Yu mother fixin brekfas."

David went into the bathroom. He was still rubbing his eyes. Glen walked back to the living room.

"Is what de two of yu was laughin bout in dere?" asked Sandra.

"Man business."

"Wha kine of man business?"

"Jus de tings a neva tell him before, cause I been away."

He had spoken without thinking and he knew it. Sandra held her head down, but Glen saw her eyes. He tried to change the subject.

"So yu guwane to market this evening? We have any money?"

"I have a likkle extra from las week. It wi do."

"Me have ten dollar me can spare."

He had blundered again. Sandra stared angrily at him as he opened his wallet and pulled out a Gordon. He saw the look on her face.

"Lawd, Sandra, yu doan tink dat I still sellin herb? Is jus dat I had some for meself and Jah-son from up Beverly Hills..."

"Yu mean de buway who father is the minister in the government. I hear him father did say him cyaan come back in de house till him shave off dem locks."

"De same one. Well, him come visit me. So I give him what me have and him give me twenty dollar. But me tell him me wasn' sellin no more. Him say him was guwane come look fa me dis mornin."

"Fa what?"

123

"Me doan know. Him just say him wan fe talk wid me. Him always full of questions, a real Benjamite."

Sandra had turned away. The thought that somehow he had slipped, that he'd gone back to what had cost him, had cost them so much, shocked her. She couldn't face him.

"Sandra, believe me, is de truth."

"Glen, I believe yu, I trus yu. Is jus that I fraid. Look how dem shoot yu up, look how much trouble we go through. Lord, Glen, I know tings rough, but we can mek it. As soon as yu get betta, yu can do anyting yu want except de business, I beg yu."

Glen held her by the shoulders and massaged the back of her neck. She made a stuttering sound as if she were about to cry. Glen tried to comfort her. He'd been truthful about everything, everything except Duffus. He hadn't told her that Duffus was coming to see him. He held Sandra close to his body, turned her around, and kissed her.

"It gettin late, go see if David ready," she said as she held his waist and pulled away. Glen returned to the room and found David struggling with the zipper on his pants.

"Hold it there, boy! I want grandchildren!"

"What, Daddy?"

"Neva mine. Twenty years from now yu wi tank me."

He helped David tuck his shirt and zipped up his pants. He noticed that David didn't have his belt.

"Where yu belt?"

David ran into the living room and brought back the belt.

"What I tell yu bout leavin yu belt inside the livin room? Yu want people to tink is pure boogoyaga live in dis house?"

"I won' do it again, sah."

"Okay."

Glen helped him with his shoes and socks, all the time looking at how tall he'd grown, glowing with admiration. Sandra called from the living room.

"Glen, David, yu brekfas' guwane col' if yu doan come now."

Father, led by son, marched into the living room and stood by the tiny area reserved for eating.

"Reporting for mess as ordered, Sergeant Ma'am," said Glen. David saluted.

"The two of yu betta sit down before I Sergeant Ma'am de two of yu."

Glen sat in his chair and drank his coffee. He watched Sandra as she served David his tea, and hard dough bread. The butter was spread thinly over the slice.

Glen touched the back of her knee.

"Glen, yu too bad!"

He smiled while David continued to eat his breakfast, oblivious to what was going on, chewing each mouthful carefully, savouring the taste of the butter.

"See that David finish him brekfas'. I guwane go get ready now," said Sandra as she loosened the tassels on the front of her nightdress. It was the same gown she had worn since she had been nursing David. "Yu still watching me, no?"

"Any law say a man cyaan look at him wife."

"If is only look him lookin."

"Any law gainst that too."

Sandra smiled and went inside the bedroom. Glen finished his coffee and went over to the front door. He opened it and looked outside. The early morning sun seared the edges of the shacks that bordered the housing project where they lived.

They had gotten the house because Glen had helped Danny steal a few ballot boxes and other odd jobs during the last election. With the money, Glen made a down payment on one of the last few completed houses in the area, which Danny had reserved for him. The contractor had run off to Miami leaving the scheme half-finished. Everyone knew how they'd gotten the house, and there was a feeling of envy and growing hatred between those who lived in shacks and those who had received the concrete houses with modern conveniences such as indoor toilets.

The shack dwellers banded together against the house dwellers. There was rarely any crossing into rival territory. Children who had gone to primary school together met only at Christmas or Easter when the Catholic brothers arranged a fair or passion play. Six months after Glen had been shot, the rector for Glen's old high school, St. George's, asked Glen to help him plan a barbecue for both communities.

"We have to do it for the children, we have to save the children," he urged.

The barbecue ended in a shoot-out, and a death threat against the rector. As each side became increasingly wary of the other, rumours circulated about beatings and even torture of those who crossed enemy lines. Both, too, had become competitors in the marijuana trade and were equally intent on keeping their share of the trade. There were no rules to the rivalry; a gun tucked in your waist was the only protection. But even this was no guarantee as Peter, one of Glen's best friends, discovered.

Even in the middle of August, Peter always wore a winter overcoat with a sawn-off shotgun tucked inside the lining. He stopped off at Kreamy Korner Ice Cream Parlour to buy an ice cream cone – the king-sized ones he loved to eat. While he sat in his car, licking the sides of the cone, and sucking off the drops that had fallen on his fingers, a car pulled up beside him and sprayed his car with three magazines from an Uzi. He never had a chance.

Glen shook his head as he looked down at the shacks. Across the river, a man about his age was trying to nail a piece of cardboard over a hole in the side of his house.

"David, yu finish eatin yet?" asked Sandra.

She had ironed her maid's uniform that the Syrian for whom she worked insisted that she wear on the job. It was neatly wrapped in a paper bag so it wouldn't be soiled on the way to work.

"Yes, Ma'am, I done."

"Go wash yu hand and come den."

David scampered to the bathroom, and Glen tiptoed behind Sandra and held her around her waist.

"So I will see yu dis evenin?" he asked.

"I know yu jus wasn' looking."

"Yu know me better than that."

"Yes, yu wi see me dis evenin."

Sandra smiled when she said this. 'Seeing' was a word they had devised for making love. They used to spell out "sex" until one day David said, "Daddy, what is S-E-X? Is the same as sex?" From then on, they began 'seeing' each other. Glen kissed them both good-bye and stood by the gate.

"Take care," he shouted.

"We will," said Sandra. David turned momentarily to wave, but Sandra gestured to him, and he began walking faster. Glen closed the door and went to the kitchen. He coughed and pulled a rag from his pocket. There were no new bloodstains. He had begun to heal.

Glen gathered the dishes from the table and filled the sink with water. He scraped the crumbs from the dishes into a paper bag he kept by the kitchen cabinet.

He washed the dishes and stacked them in a dish tray the Syrian had thrown out and Sandra had picked up from the garbage. At first, when he learned how she had gotten it, he had thrown it out of the kitchen door. But his pride soon gave way to its usefulness, and with Sandra's urging, he went outside and brought the tray back to the house before anyone else took it. The dishes sparkled just as brightly from his secondhand tray.

As soon as he was finished, Glen went inside the bedroom. Behind the foot of the bed was a small package of marijuana he had been saving for himself He took the paper out of the package, rolled a spliff, and sat on the steps. He watched John Crows flap across the sky, dipping between the tenements and the trees. No wonder the shack dwellers were so envious. From his house, he could see all of August Town, the Mona

127

Reservoir, Papine, and Hermitage down to the Dungle; each separate, busy with their own lives.

"Glen!"

"Who dat!"

"It's me, Jason."

"Forward, Jah-son."

Jason entered the yard and looked. He couldn't figure where the voice came from. Barely out of his teens, Jason was of moderate height, bowlegged and wore the beginnings of dreadlocks. Jason was living on his own. His own father had died in a car accident on Marcus Garvey Boulevard when he was only six months old. Since then his mother had re-married and as he grew older, Jason had found it more and more difficult to live under the same roof with his stepfather. He looked through the window and saw the back of Glen's head. Glen's locks trailed down his shoulders.

Jason had idolized Glen when they were both in high school. Glen had been the prefect in charge of his first form class, and Glen would take them swimming or get them passes to Manning Cup matches at the National Stadium. Before he was expelled from high school, Glen had been nominated to be the headboy of St. George's, and the principal had high hopes for him. The principal had hoped that Glen would have gone on to be a Rhodes Scholar and to revive some of the lustre that the college had lost in recent years. But the principal soon became the most vocal advocate for Glen's expulsion when he found out that Glen had gotten a girl pregnant and insisted that Glen was setting a bad example.

Glen viewed the situation differently. When he realised that Sandra was pregnant, and that her mother had thrown her out of the house and called her a whore, he did what he felt he had to do as a man and a Rastaman. He "cleaved unto his woman and the two became one flesh". Glen knew it was not the fact that he had a child out of wedlock that disturbed the principal, for if illegitimacy were a crime, then three-quarters of Jamaica would be criminals. It was when he declared himself to be a Rastaman that everyone became upset. Because of his athletic prowess and intelligence, he'd become part of their world. He had gone to their schools, gone to their parties, and spoke the Queen's English with the same nagging sense of hypocrisy that many of them had. In his case, it was a double burden, for he was a Rastaman from August Town.

"Hail, Glen."

"Ites, Jah-son. So wha de I wan' see me bout?"

Jason couldn't answer. He'd rehearsed the entire conversation in his mind, but now the words wouldn't come. He didn't know where to begin. Glen didn't want to rush him. He knew the tribulations that the boy must have been going through. It must have been difficult for Jason growing up in Beverly Hills, surrounded by maids, swimming pools, everything he wanted, and then looking down the hill, seeing all the poverty and, with all that he had, he couldn't do anything about it. Worse still, he was growing up with a step-father who didn't care or even try to understand what was going on in the ghetto. He dismissed the brethren as "thieves and hooligans" and Rastafari as a "gutter religion." He'd threatened to disown Jason, but it only served to alienate them further, for Jason knew his father had left him a portion of his estate. All he had to do was turn twenty-one. Besides, Jason had already disowned his stepfather. And as for material things...

"My stepfather and I had another fight," said Jason.

"Bout what?"

"The usual. 'After I sent you to one of the best schools in the country... bla, bla, bla'. You know, you went to St. George's too."

"Doan hole dat gainst me. It was only four years," said Glen.

"But you know what people expect?"

"No, I doan know."

Jason put his hands in his pockets and turned on the balls of his feet.

"I doan know either. But how? I mean," he stuttered. "You went through catechism and all of that. I mean, now that I'm living out here alone, everything seems so much harder. More's at stake. I mean, how, how can I be sure I'm not fooling myself? How can I be sure that Haile Selassie was God?"

"Was? His Majesty **is** God!" said Glen.

"But look how he died? They don't even know where he's buried."

"An you can tell me where Jehsus Christos or Moses was buried?"

"But he didn't do a thing for his people," said Jason. "They were starving while he lived in wealth."

"Same ting dem say bout Jehsus. Him feed seven thousand an still dat wasn't enough. When dem soldier gamble for him clothes, yu tink it was for no likkle pyan-pyan clothes. De clothes mus did good, or else dem wudn gamble fa it. Dem wud a jus throw it way. So Jehsus mus did have some corn fe spen pon clothes. Him mus did have money."

"All that is well and good, but how could Selassie be God?"

"Den what yu think? What yu want? Is a white man yu want fa God? Yu think God cud be a white man? Yu haffi get dem idea out of yu mine, Jah-son."

"But how?"

"Mek I show yu a way. Check dis out. Selassie, seen, maybe him wasn' Jah, but him look like Jah or is de closest dat mortal man will ever see of the face of Jah."

Jason shook his head and smiled. He knew the flaws of Glen's argument, but the sincerity in Glen's voice calmed his need for logic. And as far as Glen was concerned, the discussion was over.

"So, yu fine somewhere to stay yet?" asked Glen.

"I'm probably going to stay with my aunt, Mercedes. She understands me. My stepfather says I can't come back to the house until I cut off my locks."

"So yu guwane cut dem off?"

"I don't know. I miss my family. I never thought that growing locks would cause so much trouble."

"When a man decide to become a locksman, him should know dat trials and tribulations will follow him."

"But my stepfather said... "

"Forget what yu stepfather say. Who yu guwane listen to? Yu Father or yu step-father?"

"That's why I came to see you."

"Hey, me not dat old. Me was jus a few years ahead of yu. Me still a work out things jus like you. Me is still a young man."

"Yeah, it was just a couple of years ago you were at St. George's playing for the Manning Cup Team. You almost got a scholarship to the States."

"Dat was a long time ago," he said abruptly.

"And everyone thought you'd gone mad when you became Rasta."

"Who say I mad?"

"Nobody?"

"Who?"

"My fath..."

"Yeah, Mr. Minister of Justice. Jah-son, I guwane tell yu someting. Yu haffi live yu own life. Not yu father life, not yu mother life, yu own life."

"But I don't know... "

"Not even a sparrow fall from the sky without Jah know. De I worth more dan a sparrow. Trus Jah-Jah, youtman, an yu wi safe. Trus Jah Jah."

There was a knock at the gate. It was Duffus, herbsman and second only to Danny Forbes as a top ranking in the area. He was a lean man with a wispy beard and a little paunch. His neck was long and his Adam's apple protruded. Tufts of thick black hair grew on his fingers. Chickens scurried through the fence. Glen threw them a few marijuana seeds which they pecked at nervously.

"Is me, Duffus."

"I been waiting fa yu," said Glen.

Duffus shuffled into the yard, his footsteps cautious at every turn. Jason looked at him and felt uncomfortable.

"Hail, dread," said Duffus.

"Ites, Duffus. So what a go on?"

"Nothing much. Me jus come fe see the I."

Jason felt out of place. He eased over to the side of the house.

"I'll see you later, Glen," said Jason and walked through the gate.

"Ites, Jah-son," said Glen. "More time."

Duffus watched Jason's every movement. He was ready to spring into action if the boy made any sudden movements.

"Doan worry, dread, de youth naw trouble a soul," said Glen.

"Yu can neva be too sure, dread. You know dat."

"I know, I know," said Glen.

"I-man have a deal for the I," said Duffus as soon as Jason was out of the yard.

"Wha kine a deal?" asked Glen as he pulled the spliff and licked the sides of the paper, curling its ends with his fingers.

"We have good deal, man. Some boys come from Florida. Dem is right here today. One of de shipment get ketch by de coas' guard and dem need fe replace it, or some guys up in New York guwane do dem a ting. So dem check me. But you is the only one me know can put a deal together real fast, so me come check yu. Look, dem gi me de money."

Duffus flashed a bag of American dollars. Hard currency and on the black market, and they could probably be sold at forty to one Jamaican dollars.

"Is dis yu come to me yard wid dis morning. I doan tell yu I finish wid dat? After all dat happen, I doan tell yu? I-man did think is sumting sensible dat yu was a come with, some welding work or sumting like dat. Is dis me spend de hole night a worry bout? Man, just lef me alone."

Duffus stared at him incredulously. He opened the bag a little wider for Glen to get another glimpse.

"Man look at dis. Dollars, American dollars."

"Close de bag and leave me yard."

Duffus closed the bag. He knew Glen needed the money, and he had figured that just the sight of the money would be enough to convince him.

"Doan tell me is fraid yu fraid."

"Fraid? Fraid a what?"

"Den is what? We can mek some money, man. Fifty maybe hundred thousan dollars."

Glen took out a book of matches and lit the spliff.

"Look, Duffus, de last time yu come to me yard yu sey de same ting and look wha happen. Robby dead an me get shot. Yu mean yu forget wha happen so fast?"

"I doan forget, man, me doan forget. You forget who tek care of all de funeral arrangement? Who tek care of yu money for lawyer and hospital? Especially de hospital business. Eh, who? So doan tell me bout I forget. Robby dead, and we alive. Let de dead alone and enjoy yu life."

"Enjoy life! Enjoy life! Man, when yu lose a good, good friend, what else yu want? Robby wasn't even like me friend, him was me brethren. An all de killin dat go on, for what? I tired. I tired of de killin."

"But Glen, look at yu house. Yu pay out everything, sell everyting. Sandra lose all the furniture."

"And me son barely know me face," said Glen.

"Him will know yu face in time. Look, man, de only reason me tellin yu dis is because yu is me friend an me cyaan bear fe see yu live like dis when yu could be mekking good money. Dis is a one time ting, man. Might even pull off the de 'Five Bag Skank' wid dem cause I doan tink me can get enough herb together."

Glen stopped puffing on his spliff. The 'Five Bag Skank' was one of Duffus' favourite scams. He would pick five bags seemingly at random, open them, and reveal some of the reddest, seedless stalks of marijuana on the planet. The problem was at least half of the other bags were filled with mint or lower-grade marijuana.

He used this trick when the police were after him and he couldn't harvest enough marijuana from his growers. It was a risky situation, but the rewards were high, and he'd never been caught. He would be paid full price for a load when he would be delivering only half or sometimes a third of the load. By the time the smugglers realised they'd been fooled, they'd be far away and Duffus would be safe in August Town. Only a madman would try and capture Duffus in his own backyard.

"De Babylon dem, is like dem waan fe put me out a business. But you is de only one who can help me wid dis. Ranking Grip, de likkle buway who me a train, barely know de running yet."

"An yu still dealing wid Janga and Mignott? Dem same buway dat shat me, an get Robby dead."

"Is all in de business. You know dat. You get ketch, but de other shipment go through."

"All for money."

"Money is money. Me no care where it come from. All it have to say is 'In God we Trust' and I-man safe."

"Safe?" said Glen.

"Safe!" answered Duffus.

Glen stretched his legs and crossed them. He flicked ash from his spliff on the steps.

"Duffus, dem yout here a some different yout yu know. Dem likkle crack smokin', jerry curlin', walla-walla buway don't feel no pain bout just killin anybody."

"Me know, Glen. Dem soon tun like dem buway in New York or Miami, but dem fool-fool jus de same."

"Well, me friend, me nah deal wid no man that kill me friend."

"So then how me and yu stan, Glen?"

"Wha yu mean?"

"Me still a deal wid de same man dem," said Duffus.

"Dat is fa yu and dem fe work out. Me nah hole nothing gainst yu fa dat."

"Is jus so den. I man haffi go. De buway dem a wait for me."

Duffus held out his hand and Glen shook it. Duffus turned and left the yard. The gate swung noisily on its hinges. Glen sat amidst the chickens, his eyes welling with tears.

"Walk good, me brethren."

He got up from the steps and went inside. He looked around the room, and he thought he was a fool for turning down Duffus. All the furniture that remained was either cracked or broken in some way. Everything was makeshift, pieced together by his own hand. He had nothing more that could be repossessed.

He picked up the keys for the front door and decided to go for a stroll. As he walked along the street, he could see some of the older boys from the area playing soccer in the road. They stayed away from the pavement where the carcass of a dead dog had been pushed underneath a light pole. It had been there for days and flies buzzed around its head as John Crows pecked at its eyes and entrails.

Almost all of the boys were unemployed. Those that had part-time or full-time jobs had to lie about where they lived. If an employer found out they were from August Town, some reason would be invented to fire them, because everyone knew that boys from August Town were all convicted criminals. If they hadn't been convicted, it meant they hadn't been caught, yet. The boys filled their days with soccer scrimmages, playing dominoes and seducing maids and waitresses who worked uptown.

A police car cruised by, the officers watching their every movement, for it was close to Christmas, a time when young men's thoughts turned to grand theft and armed robbery.

"Burn Babylon!" the boys shouted in unison. The policemen paid no attention to them, but continued at a cautious pace. Their radio crackled. Suddenly, the driver accelerated around the corner, sirens wailing.

"I wonder where dem going?" said Glen to Ian, one of the boys.

"Jus fe fuck wid people," said Ian.

Ian had the reputation for being a gossip and a practical joker. He always wore tennis shoes and had the habit of sneaking up on girls, covering their eyes, and saying, "Guess who?" as if they didn't know from the start.

"Probably roun to Danny. Must be to check out if him still selling guns. Him have a big dance tonight, you know. De man goin?"

"I might tink bout it."

"De I fe come, man. Is a long time we no see de I. Can smoke some herb an reason. Long time I man doan reason wid de I."

"Truly," said Glen.

"So where de I a forward?" asked Ian.

"Roun to Miss Prince fe get some tea for David. Him have a col'."

"Well, if anybody can cure col', is Miss Prince."

"I know," said Glen.

"So I wi see de I tonight roun Danny?"

"I wi tink bout it."

"Awright den, Glen, more time."

"Lion, Glen, Lion!" the boys shouted. Glen waved and continued down to Miss Prince's house. She had a corner lot with a huge poinciana tree that ignited the sky. Glen knocked at the window.

"Who wee, who dat?"

"Glen!"

"I soon come, Glen. I soon come!"

The old woman hobbled to the window. She took her keys out of her pocket and opened the door. Her face was drowned in the shadow of a madras tie-head. She wore a loose-fitting old-fashioned dress and black leather sandals. Her face was gaunt and fleshless – as if the worms had already entered her body, leaving only the frame of bone under drawn skin. But her movements were sure and steady, surprising for a woman in her nineties, and her eyes were alive with a brightness that flickered from the sunken sockets.

Glen entered and was wrapped in the smell of the eucalyptus and herbal medicines Miss Prince swore had kept her alive all these years.

"I never expect to see yu here," she said.

"I come to get de tea for David," he said.

"Sandra neva tell me yu was coming for it. Is a good ting me did prepare it dis mornin."

"Me neva want she fe haffi come all di way after she come home from work. Me did want fe surprise her."

"Well, it inna de kitchen. Me have it wrap inna some grease paper. I was guwane sen me granson with it so she wudn' haffi come all dis way," she said teasingly.

Glen pursed his lips. The old woman knew he hadn't come for the tea.

"What really botherin yu, me son?" she asked.

She was the most respected woman in the area. She was probably the only person who could pass from August Town through Hermitage and Papine. Anyone who had problems could go to her with them. She was grandmother to everyone. Some of the older men called her 'Nana'. But she still kept a dead-bolt on her door.

"So what wrong, me son?"

"Miss Prince, me haffi ask yu someting."

"What, me son?"

"I hear yu can tell people what dem dream mean."

"Me never promise nothing, but tell me what yu dream."

The old woman moved closer to him. He could smell Ben Gay ointment through her blouse.

"Miss Prince, I dream, I dream, I running through the town, and not a soul aroun, and I searchin, but I don't know what I searchin for, but is only dead people keep asking me 'What yu want?' and everywhere door keep closing."

"Closing, yu say?"

"Closing, yes. It mean anything?" asked Glen.

"I doan know. But go on."

"Well, I keep searchin and de door dem keep closing and I cyaan find a soul. Neither Sandra nor David was home. Den a man call me name, an I get frighten. So I start to run, an run, til I reach de river. And de voice call me name again. Den de voice me cudn see, jump on me back an start ride me like a racehorse, and me fall down. When me look up, de man was me son, David. An him was vex. Den me wake up."

Miss Prince held his arm, her face filled with apprehension.

"An how long now yu been dreamin dis?" she asked.

"Two months now."

"De same dream?"

"Same exact."

"Hmmm. Same exact dream. For two months."

"So what it mean?" asked Glen.

Pulling her skirt between her legs, Miss Prince looked up to the ceiling. A spider in the corner of the living room was rebuilding its web.

"Dis one have me beat, me son."

"Yu mean yu cyaan tell me what de dream mean?"

"Is not that. Is jus dat de dream so full, it will take me some time to digest."

"So yu cyaan tell me, den?"

"I cud tell yu, but only in part," she said.

"Well, tell me a part."

"But de part is only part of de whole dream. An if yu jus tek out a piece, den I might mislead yu. Yu see," she paused, "a dream is like a honeycomb. Every part fit. Some part sweet, some part sour. Same way it go wid dream. I might tell yu only de sweet part, or de sour part, but yu never get de whole ting. An de whole ting yu haffi swallow whole, sweet and sour."

"So when yu cyan tell me den?"

"Maybe a month time."

"A month. Yu know what can happen in a month?"

"A whole heap a tings, me son. An den again nothing. But if me was you, me wudn really worry. For it might jus be all de poison in yu system from dem gunshot. A bullet do awful tings to a man system, yu know. Some people swell up like bull frog after a gun shot, an some maga down to a piece of stick."

"I know, look at me!"

"Bullet poisoning. Once yu get all de bile outta yu system, I bet yu any money yu soon feel betta."

"Awright, Miss Prince, if yu say so."

"Not if I say so! I know so!"

"Well, take care den, I wi see you."

"Yu forgettin de tea for David?"

Glen smiled with her and picked up the package for David and tucked it under his arm. He left a five dollar bill under a kerosene lamp.

"I will see yu den, Miss Prince."

"I wi see yu too, Glen. An doan worry, dese tings have a way of working demself out."

Glen staggered into the glare of the midday sun and faced the road. It was deserted. He laughed to himself. *Yu tek yuself too serious, Glen, too serious.* As soon as he reached home, he went straight to the bedroom and collapsed on the bed. He pulled off his shirt and immediately fell asleep, trying to remember where he'd gotten the draw of herb, and where he could get some more, for that was the only explanation for the mood that overcame him.

David! David!

Glen awakened from his dream, and the sheets were soaked with sweat. He looked around the room. No one was home.

"David? Sandra?"

He pulled on his shirt and a jacket. It was night. They should have been home already. Someone was outside, shouting his name.

"Glen! Open up quick! Is me, Ranking Grip."

139

Ranking Grip was a kid from the area who Duffus was training in the business. His real name was Ivan Smith, Jr., yet no one had ever met or known of Ivan Senior. When he started hanging out with Duffus, he worked with a reggae band and earned the nickname 'Grip'. He quit the job, and called himself 'Ranking Grip'.

"Glen, dem catch Duffus an..." Grip shouted.

Glen rushed outside fearing the worst.

"Wha happen? Wha happen to Sandra an David?"

"Doan worry bout dem. Dem at de community centre. Police block off de road."

"For what?"

"Is dat me come fe tell yu. Janga and Mignott ketch Duffus an shat him up..."

Before Grip could say anything more, Glen jumped over the fence and looked down the road.

"How it happen?"

"Him did try de 'Five Bag Skank' but it look like dem did know bout it, so dem shat him and tek way de money."

"Oh raas, not another, not again!" Glen screamed. Grip paced behind him, but Glen was determined not to hear another word. Grip ran after him and caught him by the arm.

"Glen, de two buway who shot him and tek way de money, dem inside de bar by Mr. Chen grocery store. Dem drinkin, an celebratin dat dem shat him."

Glen turned and looked at him. Grip was not thinking about the money or the herb that could have been recovered, he was thinking of getting the men. Glen could feel his anger. It was the same anger he felt when he learned Robby had died.

"Glen, them haffi pay! Dem haffi pay, man."

"Yu right, Grip, dem haffi pay. Another life nat guwane go so cheap again. Yu have a gun me can use?"

"No, all me have is de one gun Duffus give me las year. But we can go roun to Danny. Big dance tonight. Him mus have some gun underneath de big chicken coop where him always keep dem."

"Awright, wait fa me right here."

Glen jumped over his fence and dug beside one of the pillars of the house. He pulled out a plastic bag from under the dirt and opened it. Inside was an old black overcoat. He always wore the coat whenever he was going out on a job, and although it had several bullet holes, it gave him the edge he needed. As he slipped him arms through the sleeves, he realised how much his body had changed. He straightened the collar, and dusted off the sides.

They set out at a brisk pace, following the sound of the music to Danny's house. It was an old mansion built during the days of slavery. Danny had won the house in a poker game on Christmas Eve from a drunken Scotsman who later died of alcoholic poisoning.

Danny had remodeled the house. He'd hung banners of red, gold and green from a huge banyan tree which grew in the centre of the yard. The patio had been converted into a small soccer scrimmage area which the police now patrolled. Everywhere there was music, interrupted only by the sound of ciçadas, chirruping between the syncopated beats. Danny, short and squat, his eyes dark and cold like those born in the tribe of Levi, strolled by the cops and greeted them.

"Glen, yu old nayga. Long time I doan see the I. How de I feelin?"

"I man cool. I want see de I bout something. But not here. Babylon."

A woman wearing an apron with the flag of Ethiopia across its front came from the side of the house and whispered something in Danny's ear. Danny glared at the policemen and pulled away from Glen.

"Glen, me cyaan talk right now. Dem policeboy look like dem wan fuck up de dance."

"But, Danny, dis is a serious ting me come fe talk to yu bout. It cyaan wait!"

"Dis serious too, me brethren, an it cyaan wait neither! Go

roun de corner and see if yu can fine me father. Tell him what yu want."

Danny disappeared around the corner with the woman, and the policemen followed. Glen decided to check out the other side of the yard where Danny kept the chicken coop. Sitting in a circle, a group of men were passing a pipe filled with marijuana. Danny's father, an old Rastaman, presided over the circle. Jason was beside him. His eyes were heavy-lidded, and it appeared he'd been smoking all evening. Glen decided to join the circle so that he could speak to the old dread who was blessing the pipe.

"In the name of Haile I, Selassie I, Jah, Rastafar-I, Conquering Lion of the tribe of Judah."

The circle returned his blessing, "Ras-tafar-I."

Lighting the pipe, the old dread broke off his chant and puffed on the hose.

He chanted again, " Haile I, Ras, Rastafar-I."

The pipe was passed to Glen, and he pulled hard at the pipe and tried to get closer to the old dread. He passed the pipe to Jason and the pipe blazed. A few seeds burst, crackling between the men's breathing and the old man's wail. A sliver of moonlight slipped inside the yard. Jason sucked hard and filled his lungs with smoke. Holding his breath for as long as he could, he slowly let out the smoke in little puffs. His face was shrouded. He'd had too much already. The pipe made full circle and was passed again to the old dread who began his sermon. He sucked on the pipe and pointed to Jason.

"Youtman, I tell yu dis. There is one God, One Aim, One Destiny for the black man. But de children do not know this. Dere eyes see, but they are blind to the kingdom of Jah which is in their midst. For de Bible say, 'De old men shall see visions and de yung men dream, dreams.' I and I have a vision. But who shall explain de vision when dey have no teacher to teach dem?"

The dread passed the pipe to Glen and gazed up at the moon.

"Dat moon hanging over I head is Jah giving light to His

children. Dat tree growing in de middle of the yard, is Jah silent, breathing His own air, spreading to the four corners of the earth."

The pipe was passed around the circle again and all were caught in the web of the old dread's chant. Glen became oblivious to everything except the cadence of the old man's breathing.

"Dat bird flying in the sky is Jah spreading His own wings in His own sky. Dat noise under the house is Jah rubbing His legs together to make night music. Dat dog rotting in the streets is Jah giving food to His children, the John Crow."

The old dread passed the pipe again to Jason. The pipe glowed bright red, and smoke rose into the leaves of the banyan tree overhead. Jason watched the smoke rise and then his head fell to his chest.

"Those bees buzzing around the buttercups by the river is Jah, giving nectar to His children to make sweetness out of nothing. Dat river..."

"O dread, dread," Jason jumped to his feet, "I see the light, I see the light, His Majesty Emperor Haile, Selassie is God!"

Jason broke the circle and headed towards the gully. Before anyone else had realized what had happened, Glen was running after him. He knew from the signs that the boy could probably crack at any moment and feared what he'd seen happen to many uptown boys would happen to Jason. Cut off from family and friends, he'd come to the ghetto seeking groundation, only to find he was equally lost among the brethren. Left to himself, to pursue his own random thoughts, Jason could do a lot of harm to himself. Glen was the only one who would save him. Glen knew His Majesty did not come in a blinding ribbon of light. He gradually wrapped Himself in the strands of a man's hair and into his skin until He was woven into the cells of his body. As Glen started down the gully, he was met by Grip.

"Glen, me get a gun. Yu comin wid me?"

Glen looked at the boy running down the hill, out of control. He was stripping off all his clothes and tearing at his hair.

"Glen, mek we go before it too late."

"It already too late," said Glen.

Grip would have his revenge or die trying. Glen darted after Jason.

"Glen, is de last chance yu guwane get!" Grip screamed.

Glen followed Jason closely; he was just within his vision. Glen could feel fluid rising and falling within his chest. He wanted to stop, but continued running. Jason kicked off his shoes as he ran. Glen ran faster and was gaining on Jason when he turned and dashed down the hill towards the river.

"Youtman, wait!"

The boy did not hear. Glen saw the boy dive into the river. He saw his hands go up in the air. He ran faster, tore off his overcoat, and dived into the water. The boy went under, but Glen caught him as he came up.

Jason hit him in the face and went under again. Glen caught him and held him.

"Damn it man, stop it! Man, if you guwane kill yourself, go do it somewhere else. But doan do it aroun me!"

Jason struggled to be free, his hands flailing the air. Glen grabbed him and held him tightly, "Jah-son stop dis madness! Stop it! Stop it now!"

The boy stopped struggling and Glen let him go. He came up and began an awkward treading motion. He was about to go under again when Glen caught him.

"Is awright, Youtman. Is awright."

Glen lifted him and dragged him over to the other side of the river's banks.

Jason was still having trouble breathing and Glen turned him over on his chest.

Minutes passed.

"Wha happen to yu?" asked Glen

"I saw him!"

"Him who?"

"My father. My father, I saw him! He told me not to worry. To just wait. Everything would be okay." He paused. "What do you think?"

Glen did not answer. Instead, he helped Jason to his feet. He looked at the slope of the hill, lined with the boy's clothes. He gave his jacket to Jason, and they climbed the hill. The boy picked up his clothes and began dressing himself. Glen walked away, turning briefly to see if the boy was all right. He looked over the river and faced the shanties. His eyes followed the curve of the hill and across to Papine, Hermitage, Beverly Hills. The land was whole and blanketed with dew.

Geoffrey Philp was born in rural Struie in Jamaica. Like his near contemporary Kwame Dawes he attended Jamaica College.

He is the author of four poetry collections, *Exodus and Other Poems, Florida Bound, hurricane center*, and *xango music*. He has also written a book of short stories, *Uncle Obadiah and the Alien. Benjamin, My Son* is his first novel.

A recipient of many awards for his work, including an Individual Artist Fellowship from the Florida Arts Council, The Sauza Stay Pure Award, James Michener fellowships at the University of Miami, and an artist-in-residence at the Seaside Institute, he is currently working on a new collection of short stories, *Sister Faye and the Dreadlocked Vampire*. "The River" which appears in *Uncle Obadiah and the Alien*, won the Canute Brodhurst Prize from *The Caribbean Writer*. Philp's poems and short stories have also appeared in *Asili, The Mississippi Review, The Caribbean Writer, Gulf Stream, The Apalachee Quarterly, Journal of Caribbean Studies, Florida in Poetry, Wheel and Come Again: An Anthology of Reggae Poetry, The Oxford Book of Caribbean Short Stories*, and most recently, *Whispers from the Cotton Tree Root*.

Benjamin, My Son
ISBN: 1-900715-78-3; pp. 185; 2003; £8.99

Jason Stewart is in a Miami bar when he sees a newsflash reporting the murder of his politician father, Albert Lumley. With his girlfriend, Nicole, Jason returns to his native Jamaica for the funeral. There the murder is regarded by all as part of the bipartisan warfare which has torn the country apart.

But when Jason meets his old mentor, Papa Legba, the Rastafarian hints at a darker truth. Under the guidance of his locksman Virgil, and redeemed by his love for the Beatrice-like figure of Nicole, Jason enters the several circles of Jamaica's hell. The portrayal of the garrison ghetto area of Standpipe is, in particular, profoundly disturbing.

In his infernal journeyings, Jason encounters both former acquaintances and earlier versions of himself. In the process he confronts conflicting claims on his identity: the Jason shaped by the middle-class colonial traditions of Jamaica College and the Benjamin who was once close to Papa Legba.

Benjamin, My Son combines the excitement of the fast-paced thriller, the literary satisfactions of its intertextual play and the bracing commentary of its portrayal of the sexism, homophobia and moral corruption which have filled the vacuum vacated by the collapse of the nationalist dream.

Florida Bound
ISBN: 0-948833-82-3; pp. 64; 1995; £6.95

These poems of exasperation and longing explore a reluctance to leave Jamaica and the 'marl-white roads at Struie' and anger that 'blackman still can't live in him own/black land' where 'gunman crawl like bedbug'. But whilst poems explore the keeness and sorrows of an exile's memory, the new landscape of South Florida landscape fully engages the poet's imagination. The experience of journeying is seen as part of a larger pattern of restless but creative movement in the Americas. Philp joins other Caribbean poets in making use of nation language, but few have pushed the collision between roots language and classical forms to greater effect.

Carrol Fleming writes in *The Caribbean Writer*: 'His poems are as vibrant and diverse as Miami where "each street crackles with dialects/variegated as the garish crotons". Miami, albeit citified, becomes just one more island with all that is good, bad and potentially violent beset by the same sea, same hurricanes, and "mangroves lashed sapless by the wind".

"Philp's poems wander through bedrooms and along the waterfronts of that perceptive land accessible only to poets, only to those who can pull the day through dawn fog to the delicate "breath of extinguished candles".

"Philp weaves dialect and landscape into his lines with subtle authority. It is easy to get caught up in the content and miss the grace of his technique."

Hurricane Center
ISBN: 1-900715-23-6; pp. 67; 1998; Price: £6.99

El nino stirs clouds over the Pacific. Flashing TV screens urge a calm that no one believes. The police beat a slouched body, crumpled like a fist of kleenex. The news racks are crowded with stories of pestilence, war and rumours of war. The children, once sepia-faced cherubim, mutate to monsters that eat, eat, eat. You notice a change in your body's conversation with itself, and in the garden the fire ants burrow into the flesh of the fruit.

Geoffrey Philps's poems stare into the dark heart of a world where hurricanes, both meteorological and metaphorical, threaten you to the last cell. But the sense of dread also reveals what is most precious in life, for the dark and accidental are put in the larger context of season and human renewal, and *Hurricane Center* returns always to the possibilities of redemption and joy.

In the voices of Jamaican prophets, Cuban exiles, exotic dancers, drunks, race-track punters, canecutters, rastamen, middle-class householders and screw-face ghetto sufferers, Geoffrey Philp writes poetry which is both intimately human and cosmic in scale. On the airwaves between Miami and Kingston, the rhythms of reggae and mambo dance through these poems.

Xango Music
ISBN: 1-900715-46-5; pp. 64; 2001; £6.99

In the Xango ceremony, the contraries of New World African experience find transcendence. From the established, bodily patterns of ritual comes release into the freedom of the spirit; from the exposure of pain comes the possibilities of healing; and for the individual there is both the dread aloneness with the gods and the 'we-ness' of community.

Simultaneously the rites celebrate the rich, syncretic diversity, the multiple connections of the African person in the New World and enact the tragic search for the wholeness of the lost African centre. And there is the god himself, standing at the crossroads, 'beating iron into the shape of thunder', both the prophetic voice warning of the fire to command the creator who hammers out sweet sound from the iron drum.

Geoffrey Philp finds in Xango a powerful metaphor that is both particular to the Caribbean and universal in its relevance.

David and Phyllis Gershator writes in *The Caribbean Writer*: 'Using rhythm and riffs, he can pull the stops on language and give it a high energy kick. In 'jam-rock' he winds up with 'the crack of bones, the sweat of the whip; girl, you gonna get a lot of it; get it galore; my heart still beats uncha, uncha uncha, cha'.

Opal Palmer Adisa
Until Judgement Comes: Stories about Jamaican Men
ISBN: 184523 042 6; pp. 258; pub. Feb. 2007; £8.99

The stories in this collection move the heart and the head. They concern the mystery that is men: men of beauty who are as cane stalks swaying in the breeze, men who are afraid of and despise women, men who prey on women, men who have lost themselves, men trapped in sexual and religious guilt, men who love women and men who are searching for their humanity...

The stories are framed by the memories of an old Jamaican woman about the community that has grown up around her. The seven stories are structured around wise sayings that the community elder remembers as her grandfather's principle legacy, concerning the nature of judgement, both divine and human. Each story uses a saying as the starting point but the stories are far from illustrative tracts. From Devon aka Bad-Boy growing up with an abusive mother, to Ebenezer, a single man mysteriously giving birth to a child, to the womanizer Padee whose many women and children struggle to resolve issues with their father, each story reveals the complex, and often painful, introspective search of these men.

Jacqueline Bishop
The River's Song
ISBN: 978184523088; pp. 182; July 2007; £8.99

"In this moving and assured debut novel, Jacqueline Bishop sings of the everyday struggles of Gloria and her mother in their Jamaican home. *The River's Song* is a story of ambition and achievement, of the steady but troubled rise of a bright child who discovers that finding her own song could mean opposing those she most loves. *The River's Song* is tender but avoids sentimentality and at the end of the novel we find a young woman living on her own terms and following her own dreams. An engaging read. You keep leaning closer to the novel to hear every word as it is being sung."

Merle Collins

"I LOVE The *River's Song*! It was so hard to put it down! Gloria's coming-of-age story is warm and true and bittersweet. Hers is no wide bridge over the river but a rocky path to womanhood, to friendships made and lost and to the knowledge that love also requires navigation. *The River's Song* is a song we've all heard before, but never with such force and clarity as this."

Olive Senior

Kwame Dawes
Impossible Flying
ISBN: 1-84523-039-6; pp.84; 2007; £8.99

Impossible Flying is Kwame Dawes' most personal and most universal collection, that tells ' family secrets to strangers'. In exploring the triangular relationship between the poet, his father and younger brother, there are moments of transcendence, but often there is 'no epiphany, just the dire cadence of regret' since the failures of the past cannot be undone, and there is no escape from human vulnerability, and the inevitabilities of disappointment, age and death. But from that acceptance comes a chastened consolation.

As ever with Dawes's collections, the rewards come not only from the individual poems, but from their conversations and the meanings that arise from the architecture of the whole.
And as for poems themselves, 'they are fine and they always find a way to cope .../ they outlast everything, cynical to the last foot.'

Kwame Dawes
A Far Cry from Plymouth Rock: A Personal Narrative
ISBN 1 84523 025 6 £12.99

After ten years of living and working in South Carolina, of trying to manage a writing career that spans the USA, the UK and Jamaica, but of hanging onto a Ghanaian passport despite its manifold inconveniences at airport immigration desks, the question of where was home had become for Kwame Dawes ever more insistent. There is a part of him that embraces the New World condition of being Kamau Brathwaite's 'poor, harbourless spade', but America has entered his psyche; he writes poems filled with the landscapes and racial histories of South Carolina, and yet the thought of becoming an American citizen is almost too uncomfortable to contemplate.

In this deeply personal narrative, Dawes explores the experiences that bring him to this state of indecision. At its heart lies his relationship with his father, Marxist, Caribbean nationalist, writer, a relationship Dawes has explored in manifold forms in his fiction and poetry, and which in this book he approaches directly for the first time. In the process, he writes with great thoughtfulness about place (Ghana, Jamaica, Canada, the UK and South Carolina), about race, nation, religion, childhood, family and parenthood, sex and death.

As a writer, and as a husband, father, teacher, churchgoer and community activist, and one sees that for Dawes the page and the world, cannot be divided. If, in the end, there is a conclusion, it is about embracing the abrasions and joys of difference. In a world where the pressures to homogenise are so great, one realises just how important it is that there are writers like Kwame Dawes around.